Jet Tagasa is a former OFW and broadcast media professional. She lived and worked in Hong Kong and Dubai for over two decades, from 1996 to 2018. In 2019, she settled back in Manila, alongside her husband and two cats. When she's not weaving spine-chilling stories, Jet unleashes her creative energy as an events creative in Manila, Philippines. Her inaugural literary venture, *The Secret Lives of OFWs*, opens a new chapter in her storytelling journey.

The Secret Life of OFWs

Jet Tagasa

PENGUIN BOOKS

An imprint of Penguin Random House

PENGUIN BOOKS

Penguin Books is an imprint of the Penguin Random House group of companies whose addresses can be found at global.penguinrandomhouse.com

Published by Penguin Random House SEA Pte Ltd
40 Penjuru Lane, #03-12, Block 2
Singapore 609216

First published in Penguin Books by Penguin Random House SEA 2025

ISBN 9789815204858

Typeset in Garamond by MAP Systems, Bengaluru, India

www.penguin.sg

Contents

Author's Note

To be honest, I did not begin *The Secret Lives of OFWs* with the intention of writing a horror book. Sadly, however, many of the circumstances that have inspired these stories are horrific in nature. So horrific that I wanted to change the narrative. Even if it's only in fiction. I think of it as a way of processing my repulsion at the unfortunate circumstances some of our *kababayans* have endured, and continue to do so, just so they can provide for their families and have a better life.

So, I confront horror with horror and writing about it has been immensely satisfying. Kind of like watching some of the worst people you can imagine finally get what they deserve. I hope you get the same kind of feeling or satisfaction from reading this book or, at least, get a better sense of the admirable strength, immense capacity for love, and the almost superhuman resilience of many OFWs. They really are heroes, in more ways than one.

Over the years, learning about their stories ignited the spark that kicked off my journey of writing this collection. I can't recall exactly when I first started working on *The Secret Lives of OFWs*. All I know for sure is that I began when I was an OFW myself. I started with the story 'The Domestic Helper' followed by 'The Waiter'. After that, I'm unclear about which story came after what.

Many of these stories started as anecdotes or urban legends that other people either told me over a few drinks or, as I would oftentimes imagine, were whispered to me in my sleep by the phantom forms of the very creatures I've written about. I like to think that they've somehow chosen me to write their stories in the hopes that by doing so, they will be able to transcend the barrier between the fictional and mythic and real life. But, perhaps, that's another book for another day.

Ultimately, however, it's the horrors of real life that have become a macabre muse of sorts for me. Two stories in this collection have been inspired by true crime events. A fascination I have turned into a podcast called *The Last 24 Hours*. Pardon the shameless plug but if you're curious to know more about the real-life background behind some these stories, check out the podcast. It's available on all podcast platforms.

The first of these grim real-life incidents occurred in Hong Kong, in November 2014. According to news reports, a British banker went on a violent, drug fuelled killing spree that claimed the lives of two unfortunate Indonesian girls.

There were so many grotesque details about this story that would give anyone nightmares for days and perhaps influence a better writer to write their own take. Two specific details led me to eventually tell the story of 'The Part-Timer'; the presence of sex toys at the crime scene and the fact that the killer himself had called the police to report his coked out, grisly crime spree. When I first heard about the incident, I remembered thinking, *What would make a man in the middle of a killing spree do that?* It seemed as if other unexplained forces were involved.

I followed that question like it was an elusive pink bunny and it led me to create one of my favourite characters in this collection.

The second true crime event that inspired possibly one of my favourite stories in this anthology happened in Cyprus in 2019 when several migrant women and their children were murdered over a span of two years. The incident kicked off a heated national debate about how the country's treatment of female migrant workers created a situation that resulted in multiple victims and introduced Cyprus to its first known serial killer. Four out of seven victims were from the Philippines.

I immediately thought of victim's families and their parents in particular. It made me think of the fathers and mothers who have received the unthinkable news of their children's death while working abroad and the breadth of that heartbreak makes me emotional even now. I can't imagine how a normal person would survive such devastation. To be able to carry that pain and move on must require superhuman strength. This speculation led me to create the story of 'The Cook'.

Finding the information I needed regarding the creatures themselves required a combination of online and offline resources. While there is a lot of information out there, I found that the most concise and helpful online resource on Philippine folklore and mythology was Jordan Clark's 'The Aswang Project'. I supplemented my online research with information from Wikipedia and Esquire Philippines. Curiously, my online research has led me to a book by a Jesuit priest named Father Frank Lynch, who published a book in 1949 called *An Mga Asuwang: A Bicol Belief*. Digging deeper, I discovered that Father Lynch was also a professor of Anthropology and Sociology at Ateneo De Manila University, and he wrote the book based on stories and observations from locals when he was posted in Bicol.[1] Some believe that a lot of the popular literature on aswangs originated from the book and studies of Father Lynch, including the books of known aswang folklorist Maximo D. Ramos.

Offline, I gathered a lot of information and inspiration from the following books: *The Creatures of Philippine Lower Mythology* and *The Aswang Complex in Philippine Folklore*, both by Filipino writer and educator Maximo D. Ramos. Ramos is considered by many to be the 'Dean of Philippine lower mythology'. Additionally, a highly informative book by Narciso C. Tan on pre-Christian Philippine tribal practices called *Púgot : Head Taking, Ritual Cannibalism, and Human Sacrifice in the Philippines* has been particularly effective in stoking the sinister imagination that led to the creation of the Aswang cult featured in my stories. I've been fortunate enough to be able to access all these books at The Filipinas Heritage Library at the Ayala Museum.

While I've mostly adhered to commonly known characteristics of the creatures found in my book, aswang purists might discover that I've taken a few creative liberties with some of their behaviours, strengths, and weaknesses. I've done this because I'd like to think that, like many things in this world, aswang's too can evolve. Like the OFWs you are about to meet, these supernatural creatures also evolve in order to survive, and when they do, we're rewarded with stories that will, hopefully, help us overcome some of the horrors of everyday life.

---

[1] May, Glenn Anthony. 'Father Frank Lynch and the Shaping of Philippine Social Science', *Itinerario*, 22, no. 3 (1998): 99–121. https://doi.org/10.1017/S0165115300009621

THE
HOL'
BIE

The Domestic Helper

Saudi Arabia

What surprised her the most was that they tasted the same.

She should have known. After all, blood is blood, and it always speaks the truth. She scooped a palmful of his blood into her mouth and it revealed to her . . . that this fat, repugnant, hairy excuse for a human being really was no different from the helpless farmers she would feed on back home. Although, she had to admit, the farmers tasted better. Sweet and clean, like newly plucked fruit.

She suddenly felt sick. What would Papay think of her if he saw her now? The thought of his disapproval made her weep. Then, as if she was back in Banuang Gurang again, she started to hear the sound his voice.

'*Blessed is the man who endures trials,*' he boomed in her head. '*Because when he passes the test, he will receive the crown of life that He has promised to those who love Him. Remember this from the holy book, Estelita.*'

How could she forget? She'd heard this verse recited to her every day since she was a child. It was carved in her brain. A prayer that she would say to herself whenever the urges began to take hold. In fact, the phrase kept repeating inside her head as she gouged into *Amo*'s chest with her bare hands to get to his pounding heart. Despite her shame, the terror coursing through his heart tasted delightful. So, she wept and fed.

Then, she thought of coming home. The memories unfolded like a movie, showing her the past and all the inevitable choices that had led her to this very moment.

She had to leave for the Middle East. There had been no other choice.

At first, she and her father had managed to live off the land while she fed on villagers from distant, remote barrios. This had been the most important commandment of all. 'As sacred as the other ten commandments, Estelita,' her father had said. She'd known this to be the sacrosanct rule ever since her mother died and the gift passed on to her. 'Never in our own backyard, ever!' Papay had added with dramatic seriousness.

'Because wealth and riches are in His house, Estelita. Our house and Banuang Gurang. This is where His righteousness will reside and endure forever. Remember that from Psalms 112:3. So, our home, and everything surrounding it, should never be tainted by sin'. Her father always had a handy Bible verse for any conversation or situation—almost always from The Book of Psalms, his favourite.

He should have been a priest. He had wanted to be one when he was younger. The first time she had asked him why he hadn't pursued priesthood, he had simply said, 'God had other plans for me,' and ended it at that. He never liked talking about what had stopped him from going to a seminary. Estelita suspected it had something to do with her mother, but she'd never been able to talk to him about her; at least, not without her father falling into a deep sadness. She could never stand seeing him like that, so she seldom, if ever, asked about Mamay.

Estelita never did commit the sin of tainting their home by feeding anywhere close to Banuang Gurang. She feared losing the love of God too much to do so. More than that, she feared losing the love of her father. This meant that if he told her to never do one thing or to do another, especially when it came to her 'gift', she listened and did as she was told.

Occasionally, however, a local pregnant woman tested her willpower. But she had known better than to indulge in her favourite treat. Her father would have already made arrangements to protect the families. First, he would regularly drop by, under neighbourly pretences, with a bunch of garlic to hang around their house. Then, he would tell them stories of recent aswang sightings along with emphatic warnings to be extra vigilant.

'Lock your doors and windows. One can't be too careful these days!' he would say. Of course, he would leave them with a Bible verse to further add seriousness to his visits. His favourite verses would come, like always, from the Psalms. 'Let those who love the Lord hate evil. For He guards the lives of His faithful ones and delivers them from the hands of the wicked'. Estelita liked remembering him like that. Surrounded by a rapt audience as he delivered those verses. In his element. Even if she was now the very evil that he used to warn people about. No matter, those visits worked like a charm. Back then, people had been afraid because, back then, people believed.

But those days were long gone. With time, people had stopped talking about her kind under terrified hushed breaths. 'Aswang na Layog' or Manananggal, as she was known to them. There had been a time when they didn't even dare to say it. As if the mere mention of her name was enough to conjure her out of air and invite an attack. Now, those people were gone, along with the once fertile land and their way of life. Too many failed harvests and a dwindling interest in agriculture had driven their neighbours to sell their land and move to bigger towns. Nowadays, the children of farmers had moved on to become accountants, engineers, or nurses. No one aspired to live off the land any more. Now, it was all about having a professional career, going abroad, or becoming a TikTok influencer. Only the truly stubborn had stayed.

Unfortunately for her amo, her father wasn't around to hang garlands of garlic around his palatial villa for protection. There was no one to warn him about the unimaginable nightmare that he had allowed into his house and into his life. To clean after him, cook his meals, serve his wife, and look after his newborn child.

It made Estelita think about her own decisions. If someone had told her that she would be feeding thousands of miles away from home, would she have believed them? If someone had warned her of the suffering and the numbing loneliness she would eventually endure after coming here, would she have left? She was not sure of the answer any more.

Estelita spat a gobful of Amo's blood on the floor, which was muddled thick with his skin and guts and winced at the sudden acrid aftertaste of his nightly whisky and shisha habit. It tasted like his breath, like poison and decay.

The first time he had come stumbling into her room, he was shrouded in the sweet smell of apples. '*Jameela*,' he had called to her by the doorway. (She would later learn that 'jameela' meant 'beautiful' in Arabic. *A lovely word for the barbaric act that followed it*, she thought.) Then, he threw his sloppy weight on top of her before she could defend herself. Every part of her died underneath his greedy, drunken desire that night. His assault broke her body down to a husk, emptying her of soul and thought. When he left, the smell of apples hung fetid in the air.

She could tell Madam recognized the rancid spectre of her husband when she barged into Estelita's room later that morning. She sensed Madam's rage slow to shock at the crumpled sight of her and watched Madam's eyes land on the unmistakable bloodstain on the sheets.

'Why are you still in bed?!' *She knew.* Estelita had been certain. She could hear the pained dismay creeping up Madam's throat.

'Get up and make breakfast!' Madam added, this time, almost choking on her words. Then, she quickly turned to slam the door shut before Estelita could even get up.

Once she was in the kitchen, she waited for Madam to confront Amo. Dead certain that she would come down on him with fury and rage and show her wrath over his sickening action. Instead, Madam demanded she cook her foul and scrambled eggs and then yelled at Estelita to make a pot of coffee for Amo. Estelita watched him drink from his cup, while the source of her gift, an obsidian stone passed on to her by her mother, churned with rage deep in the pit of her gut.

Later that night, she dreamed of unfolding her wings under the transforming light of the full moon, of dragging their screaming, disbelieving bodies out under the night sky before tearing their hate out of their flesh and eating her revenge. But instead, she did what she had been hired to do. She quietly retreated to the routine of looking after—what turned out to be—the real monsters in her life.

It wasn't always like this. When she first arrived in Saudi, she was working for an Arab household that treated her like a human being. She had worked within the hours indicated in her contract and enjoyed weekend breaks. Best of all, she was able to satiate her urges with the fresh animal entrails and blood that she would buy whenever they would go food shopping. Her employers never thought anything of it. They trusted that she was using the meat to make the delicious meals she made for them. Which, as luck would have it, consisted of a lot of beef and lamb. Estelita made the most of it, even as she loathed the taste of dead meat.

'It worked Papay!' she proudly beamed to him on a video call after her first full moon without an incident in Saudi.

'Praise be to God!' he exclaimed in response. 'Of course it worked! Remember what the holy book says! Trust in the Lord and do good! Dwell in the land and enjoy safe pasture. Take delight in the Lord, and He will give you the desires of your heart!'

Praise be indeed. God had helped, yes, but she had also trained her urges to accept the consumption of dead meat for months before leaving for Saudi. Estelita had considered it an integral part of her preparation. To her, it had been similar to the training she received for domestic work at the Training Institute where she learned how to change diapers or cook Arabic food. Except, with this training, she knew she could ward off her full moon transformations without fresh human meat. She may not be at full capacity—as she would normally be—but at least she would be functional.

'It's going to be okay, Papay.' She remembered how good it had felt to finally tell him that.

They'd heard the horror stories; they were not naive. Estelita knew that that deciding to leave home and work in a strange foreign country was like pointing a loaded gun at yourself, pulling the trigger, and hoping that there was no bullet in the barrel. Which was why she made sure to do her due diligence when signing up with a legitimate agency. She started by making sure that the agency was accredited and even looked at the agency's reviews and testimonials from other OFWs. Estelita had been determined to be fully prepared.

A week after working for her contracted employers in Riyadh, Estelita felt confident that she had done the right thing. For a while, it had seemed like everything was going to work out just fine. Then, one day, her amo, Madam Farah, had approached her about 'briefly' moving to another household. Her sister, she claimed, who just had a baby had lost their Vietnamese domestic helper due to health reasons. Estelita couldn't say no. Even when she knew that the request was a violation of the conditions of her contract that prohibited employers from asking her to work for anyone else, she had no cause to think that her situation was going to be any different from her current experience. Besides, Madam Farah promised her that she would only be with her sister for a few months, just until her sister found a new housekeeper.

She'd been working for this new family for a month now. It felt like it had been a year.

It started with the food. Her new amos never wanted anything cooked. Their meals, with the exception of breakfast, was always delivered and always fried. When Estelita had volunteered to make them lamb kabsa, Madam had looked at her as if she'd just said the most disgusting thing and had told her not to bother. 'Just clean, clean, clean,' she had insisted, 'and then wash baby, okay?'

Estelita did as she was told but began to feel uneasy. One day, exhausted from hours of cleaning the five-bedroom villa, she returned to her room to realize that her mobile phone and passport were missing. She knew Madam had been inside. She could still smell her in the air. However, when Estelita asked Madam about it, she became indignant to the point of hysteria. 'You don't need your phone or your passport!' she screamed in Estelita's face. Estelita was too tired to react. In fact, after days of not having had any meat, she was too exhausted to even think. She only knew she had to have something fresh and soon.

One night after this incident, she tried to leave the house after the couple went to bed but had then discovered that the door to her room was locked from the outside and the gates secured by a padlock. She had to climb out of one the windows to find this out. Hungry and weary, she stood, surrounded by tall concrete walls in the middle of a well-manicured garden when it finally dawned on her—she had become her employer's prisoner. She heard Papay's voice in her head almost immediately. He said, '*He upholds the cause of the oppressed and gives food to the hungry. The Lord sets prisoners free.*' Estelita looked up at the quarter moon in the clear night sky and prayed.

Later that week, it seemed that God had answered her prayers. It happened on a Saturday. She was in the master bedroom on the second floor, scrubbing the tiles in Madam's bathroom, when she heard voices of children echoing from the ground floor. Then, a familiar voice called out to them, 'Abdul! Stop chasing after your brother!'

Estelita's pulse quickened. *It's Madam Farah! She's come to collect me back!* she had thought and immediately stopped what she was doing. Estelita was about to call to her when, suddenly, the breathless figure of Amo appeared in front of her. Like a white wall, his overweight figure had blocked the doorway of the bathroom. He placed his hand over Estelita's mouth before she could utter a word and pushed her inside.

'Shut up!' he whispered. Estelita could feel his heart struggling from suddenly exerting itself. *Madam Farah must have dropped by unexpectedly, surprising them with an unannounced visit.*

'Don't yell, don't scream. You are not here.' His hand was sweating over her mouth. She tasted the salt on her lips.

She struggled under his hold.

'If you do anything, I will make you regret it,' he hissed. But Estelita wasn't afraid of the pain he promised.

'If you get me in trouble, I'll make sure that you don't get paid. You won't see a cent, you understand me? I'll get you thrown in jail. You won't see your family ever again!'

Estelita looked into his eyes and saw that future. Frightened, she forced herself to relax. She sat on the edge of the tub and did as she was told. She was afraid, you see. But not for the reasons you might think. She owed it to Papay, who mattered above all else. Even more than ending her sick debasement.

'You are more than this,' he had always said to her. 'The good book says that those who live according to the flesh have their minds set on what the flesh desires. But those who live in accordance with the Spirit have their minds set on what the Spirit desires. So, you see Estelita, what you turn into does not define who you are; it's what's in your spirit!

Oh, but it does.

Of course, she had never contradicted him. He had worked too hard to make sure she had a different life as a viscera sucker than her uneducated mother. Unlike her Mamay, she had gone to school and even had friends. On the surface, she seemed like any other normal, young lass from Donsol (albeit more attractive than most). Except, she had never been normal. During her full moon hunts, she was terror incarnate. A merciless winged creature ingrained in the collective nightmares of all who grew up on the myth of her existence. She had never known fear. She never had to be afraid of anything or anyone. Until, of course, she learned about leukaemia.

When she learned of Papay's diagnosis, all her perceived infallibility drained away from her body. His disease stripped her to the core and showed her who she really was. Just another helpless daughter. No different from the pathetic quivering victims she would feast on. This was when she learned about real fear. The fear of mounting medical bills for treatments, laboratory tests, and medicines that they could never afford. The fear of not being able to save the bedrock of her life, her family, her everything. Estelita realized her 'gift' meant nothing. She was nothing. So, when she saw the poster for an agency looking for domestics in Saudi at the Banuang Gurang market, she rolled the dice and started planning. Estelita applied the same determination to looking for work abroad as she did to stalking and consuming a prey . . . with ruthless, single-minded purpose.

The moon, however, would not let her true nature come to pass.

She picked Amo's carcass clean of all its delectable parts and relished the sensation of power coursing through her body once more. Every morsel of his worthless flesh was restoring the life he had violated out of her. Estelita had to correct herself, maybe . . . maybe he wasn't that worthless after all. Almost instantly, she started thinking about how delectable his newborn child would taste. She salivated at the thought and absently licked her lips. An instinctive reaction she had tried for years to control, along with the deep remorse that followed it. 'I'm sorry, Papay,' she said regretfully and, with that, the floodgates opened. She wept to the point of wailing. In between mournful whimpers, she thought back to the phone call she had finally been able to make.

As the moon had moved closer to its full cycle, Estelita's body had started preparing itself for the hunt and the feed. Despite not having consumed fresh meat in weeks, she had become sharper and stronger. She knew her hunger could no longer be denied. Amo did not know why he so easily agreed to let Estelita call her father. Under the full moon's power, she was alluring, hypnotic, and undeniable beyond explanation. This time, she smelled him long before he showed up at her door. She heard his heart pounding with lustful anticipation, his blood rushing ahead of himself. Estelita met him in the doorway of her room and commanded him to get her phone for her. He did as he was told. She watched him shuffle his way back to the master bedroom where Madam was sleeping deeply. She did not stir even when Amo started looking through her things. When he found Estelita's phone, he handed it to her quietly and then remained standing by the doorway in a trance—like a pet, waiting for its next command.

When the phone rang on the other side of the world, and the call connected, the voice that greeted her was not the voice she had expected to hear. Her neighbour, Tyang Basyon, sounded both angry and relieved.

'Where have you been? We've been trying to reach you for weeks!'

'I've been . . .' she hesitated, not quite knowing what to say, '. . .working,' she finally managed.

'Where's Papay? Is he asleep? Why are you taking his call?'

Tyang Ba started to cry. 'He was asking for you a lot', she blubbered. 'I'm so sorry, Tellie.' Estelita felt her throat tighten. 'Where is he? Please, I need to talk to him,' she begged Tyang Ba.

'We tried getting in touch with you, but your phone has been off.' Tyang Ba hesitated before finally saying the words.

'He's gone.'

Estelita felt tears roll down her cheeks as Tyang Ba's voice trailed off on the line. Estelita heard her mention the time and date of his passing but through the haze of grief, she could understand nothing.

She had failed.

How could this have happened? Didn't the scriptures promise that if she endured all this pain, if she sacrificed everything and suffered through it all, she would reap the rewards of heaven? Heaven for her was a place where Papay would recover. Then, once he recovered and after her Saudi contract ended, she would come home with enough money saved up to get their house fixed. Perhaps even revive their small abaca business. She could make those pretty native bags—the ones her friends thought she made so well. She believed in this heaven because Papay had believed in it. He had always assured her that if you always do what's right, you will be rewarded in the Kingdom of God.

But now Papay was gone, and he had left her behind to save herself. Had it all been a lie? Estelita couldn't help but feel that she'd been cheated. She felt that all her sacrifices had been for nothing. God didn't care. She glanced at Amo still standing like a stunned animal in her doorway and thought, *God is dead.*

Her rage began to build and the stone in her gut set in motion its familiar twist. Estelita felt it expanding, flattening into a sharpened blade against her insides. Then, it began to spin and cut through her, breaking skin. It had been so long that the pain was almost a relief. Estelita smiled to herself and thought that even when nothing made sense, it comforted her to know that there were things she could still count on happening.

Tyang Ba's small and frantic voice called out to her on the phone. 'Hello?! Hello?'

She found that she was no longer afraid. She wiped away her tears and welcomed the sensation of her wings that began to shift and tear their way out of her back.

'What are you going to do? Can you come home?' Tyang Ba asked.

Estelita led Amo deeper into her room and instructed him to close the door behind him. 'Yes,' she said calmly. *But first, I'm hungry and my meal is waiting.* 'I will call you back, Tyang Ba.'

Estelita ended the call.

Four days later, Estelita found herself in a safe house for abused domestics like her. They came from so many different countries. Kenya, Ethiopia, Sri Lanka, and Bangladesh—women of different colours and languages unified by a profound understanding of one thing, oppression.

She shared a large room with bunk beds with three other women—a very young girl from Sri Lanka named Anitha and two other Filipinas, Gigi from Bulacan, and Vhem from Cotabato. Despite having known each other for only a short period of time, she quickly developed a friendship with her fellow kababayans. She discovered that shared trauma could do that. Their common stories of abuse acted like a bond, made sacred by the blood they shed working for their employers. Anitha, the young Sri Lankan girl, however, mostly kept to herself. She had arrived not long after Estelita and had since been curled up in one of the bottom bunk beds. She had come in the dead of night with one of the case workers and slept for what seemed like two whole days.

Gigi was the first one to talk about her during breakfast one morning.

'We should bring her some bread and eggs when we go back to the room. The poor girl hasn't eaten anything at all!'

They all nodded in quiet agreement.

'I wonder what happened to her?' Estelita asked.

'I know,' Vhem piped up. 'We have the same case worker. She told me that Anitha came from the hospital. She was found bleeding outside the emergency ward after she was dropped off by a young-looking male who took off before they could find anything out. She had blood coming down her legs and was near death.' Vhem was beginning to get choked up. 'Those fucking savages! She got pregnant by one of her employer's teenage sons and when they found out, they tried to abort the baby by sticking a steel pipe inside her!'

Gigi and Estelita squirmed.

Vhem continued. 'Lucky for her, one of the nurses quickly identified that she was being abused and called the safe house before getting the police involved.'

'Thank God.' Gigi made the sign of the cross.

'Yes, thank God,' Estelita responded, a thought beginning to form in her mind.

'What about you Tellie? How did you finally escape your employers?' Estelita turned to Vhem who had asked the question and wondered how she would react if Estelita told tell her the truth.

Would her horror of what happened to Anitha pale in comparison to the horror she had inflicted on Madam after she finished with Amo? Would Vhem still want to be friends with her if she told her what she had to do to get away?

Estelita thought back to that night once more. The night she had found out about her father's death. The night she had lost her anchor and had become helplessly and hopelessly unmoored.

After picking through Amo, Estelita realized that she wasn't satisfied. She wanted more, and she wanted good, unspoiled meat. So, she made her way to the nursery and grabbed Madam's sleeping one-year-old from his crib. She took the child with her into the master bedroom, where she woke Madam with the gusts of wind from her imposing wings.

Estelita relished the memory of Madam shrinking back in abject terror at the sight of her. The woman recoiled violently, twisting herself in such a way that it looked as if she would crawl and hide inside the mattress. This time, however, she could not hide from what was about to come.

'Did you know what your husband was doing to me?' Estelita asked while she cradled Madam's sleeping baby in her arms. 'Why did you let him do it? Why didn't you stop him?'

Madam was too stunned to respond. It was only after Estelita opened her mouth and lowered her long tongue inside the baby's navel that she started to scream.

Estelita consumed the child in front of her. Siphoning off every ounce of flavourful viscera inside his tiny young body with a hunger so quick and furious that the child wasn't even been able to cry out. By the end of it, Estelita cradled a lump of skin, hanging off infant bones.

Madam was still screaming when Estelita finally descended on her.

'And the wicked will be no more, though you look for them, they will not be found,' Estelita boomed, thinking of her father. Then, she silenced Madam's screams inside the embrace of her wings, turning her cries into the muffled breaking of skin and bones.

Estelita then spent over two days cleaning up. She mopped, washed, scrubbed, and disinfected every corner of the house, as if she was erasing every trace of the family out of existence. Then, after she was satisfied with her work, she went online and sent an SOS to a safe house. Soon after, a case worker had got in touch with her, and they made arrangements to meet up early one morning just a few blocks from the family villa. Estelita carried nothing with her except a small King James Bible that she hid from her employers by secreting it away in the back of her underwear drawer.

'Thank God you managed to escape!' she remembered the case worker exclaiming with genuine relief. Estelita hugged her and began to weep. 'Thank the Lord, it's over,' she sobbed.

Back in the kitchen, Estelita finally responded to Vhem.

'I got lucky. I managed to escape when my employers suddenly left the villa, leaving me on my own. I thought that was my chance! Probably my only chance, so I quickly got in touch with Miss Grace.'

Vhem smiled. 'Isn't she nice? I'm so glad there are people like Miss Grace in the world!'

'I'm so glad were all safe,' Gigi added. 'At least, all of us who are here . . .'

They looked each other silently. They knew they were the lucky ones.

When all three girls returned to their room, they were surprised to see Anitha sitting up on her bed. She had the sheets draped over her head. Estelita thought they made her look like the Virgin Mary.

'Hello, Anitha! It's so good to see you awake' Gigi went over to sit next to her. 'How are you feeling?'

'She's probably hungry,' Vhem quipped.

Anitha managed a weak smile and nodded.

'We'll get you food from the kitchen, don't worry!' Vhem was about to rush out when Gigi volunteered to go with her to help her. Estelita sat next to Anitha after both girls disappeared. She noticed how small she was, almost like a child. After a while, Estelita watched Anitha's hands move to her belly and linger there, like she was feeling for something.

'Everything is okay now.' Estelita didn't really know if that was the truth, but she didn't really know what else to say either. What words can you offer to take away the agony of something so horrific?

Anitha looked at her with weary eyes. 'No more baby.' She started to cry. 'I lost my baby'

Estelita wrapped her in her arms and wept with her.

'They took my baby,' Anitha whimpered and buried her head deeper in Estelita's chest. Then, as if Papay had whispered the phrase to her himself, she heard the words in her head and knew instantly what she must do.

'Anitha, the Lord is close to those who are broken-hearted and saves those who are crushed in spirit.'

The young girl turned to look up at her.

'Your baby is with the Lord now. I know it's painful and hard right now but if you believe and follow the word of God, He will give you strength. He can take away this pain and He will make sure that what you're going through will not be in vain.'

Anitha wiped away her tears and began to anticipate Estelita's next words.

'Now let's pray for the people who did this to you . . . let's pray that the Lord will take their wickedness away.' Estelita beckoned Anitha to kneel with her.

'Then, after we pray, tell me where they live,' she said and made the sign of the cross.

The Balikbayan

Hong Kong

Si Asuang . . . Si Asuang . . . Si Asuannggg!

The chanting echoed and reverberated inside Jennie's head, waking her up. As soon as she opened her eyes, she felt a sickening pressure begin to snowball inside her head. It immediately made her want to throw up. Her stomach began to churn violently, and she shot up from her bed as soon as she felt a vile thing inside her start to claw its way out. She didn't get far. Even before she could manage a few steps, she lurched over and discharged a slurry of vomit on the floor. It landed with a nauseating splat, which almost triggered her gag reflex again. By the time she felt another wave of nausea come on, she had thankfully managed to make it to the toilet. For a few agonizing minutes, Jennie emptied her insides into the toilet bowl until all that was coming out of her mouth were spit and bile.

What in the fuck did I have last night?! she thought to herself. Not that she could make anything out in the dark slush of vomit covering the rim of the bowl. It looked like a small animal had exploded in there; she shivered at the sight of it.

It made her want to swear off drinking again and mean it this time. Also, it smelled repulsive. An image of a marble table filled with decomposing meat flashed in her mind. Instantly, the small muscles in her stomach began to quiver and she instinctively reached for the toilet handle to flush the sick away. That was when she remembered that her toilet didn't flush. Her heart sank. She was going to have use a Tabo or, in this case, empty out one of the large plastic water containers positioned next to the toilet to wash it down. 'Shit,' she muttered under her breath.

Everything was beginning to come back to her now. She was in It-Ba, Philippines; her mother's hometown in Albay. And last night, her mom's family had thrown her a party. Or had they? There had been a festival, they were definitely celebrating something. They had called it the Halia or the Midnight Halia? Jennie had arrived from Hong Kong the day before and intended to stay a few days. Right now, however, the non-flushing toilet situation was making her reconsider her plans. She suddenly remembered how her mother would threaten to send her to this very town when she would get into trouble in school, which had been often. But she got it now—the threats made sense. She was not surprised at all that her mom had left all those years ago to search for a better life. It-Ba was small, remote, and very rural. It couldn't have been easy, leaving all you know and love behind, but she couldn't see her glamorous mother spending the rest of her life here either. Not when she was such a talented singer.

Anyone who ever heard her mother sing always commented on how she sounded just like Whitney Houston or Celine Dion. In fact, people would always ask her to cover 'Saving All My Love for You' or 'The Power of Love' when she used to perform at the lobby lounge of The Heritage in Tsim Sha Tsui. This was how her mother met her father. Her mother sang while her father, a talented musician himself from Pampanga, played either the piano or the guitar. They got married at the Hong Kong City Hall and made loving, harmonious music together for a year until Jennie was born. Then, one day, her mother found out from a mutual friend that her father was having an affair with one of their 'fans'—a Chinese lady who never missed a set and always asked her to sing a Celine Dion song. At some point, she discovered that they used the Celine songs as a way of sending messages to each other about where they could secretly meet. If she asked for 'Because You Loved Me', it meant they could meet up at their usual Wan Chai love motel. If she asked for 'It's All Coming Back to Me Now', they would meet at her place in Jordan. Jennie actually thought it would have been clever if it wasn't so diabolical. Over time, her mother would find out that he had been cheating on her with more than one woman. The first time she confronted him about the song request affair, it kicked off one of their many heated verbal—that eventually turned physical—fights. Her mom would always end up with a black eye or a split lip, while her dad would always storm out of their cramped studio only to return a few hours later, drunk and remorseful. She always took him back. Always.

Jennie never really understood why her mom tolerated his behaviour for as long as she did. It annoyed Jennie that her mother loved her father as much as she did. And she disdained the embarrassing lengths her mother went to, to hold onto him as if he was the only man in the world. Especially when, in her prime, Jennie's mother was this talented, attractive woman who could basically have any man she wanted. Ultimately, her mother discovered that the only way she could cope with his incessant infidelities was by becoming an alcoholic. Her poison of choice was vodka. In the end, her father decided to live with a mistress in Macau and the abandonment proved to be too much for her mother. She died of liver failure months later. When Jennie received the death certificate, the cause of death was listed as liver cirrhosis. She thought it should have said, 'suicide by Stoli'. 'Take me back home,' her mother had said to her before she finally gave in. But it would take Jennie a few months before she made good on her final wishes.

After she took her mother's ashes back to their Hong Kong flat, she stayed in bed for a week where she alternated between feeling sorry for herself and feeling angry. Anger eventually won out. How could it not? Her parents themselves had planted that seed in her. She carried it in her gut like a poisoned pit that she nurtured and watered with booze, drugs, and casual hook-ups. That's when she met Brian. A lanky third culture kid with bad tattoos and well to do parents. His family was originally from New Zealand but—like Jennie—he'd been born and raised in Hong Kong. It was not anything like true love, but it always felt like love at first sight whenever she would snort her share of his cocaine. Plus, he was a decent guitar player and when they were not too blasted, they liked jamming with each other now and then. If she wasn't such a mess, she would have likely recommended him to her bandmates. If she'd still been in the band that is. Unfortunately, she had been kicked out of the group after an unfortunate on-stage urination incident.

Months into her downward spiral, her mother started coming to her in her dreams. At first, she would appear to Jennie as she had been on her deathbed, withered and yellow, beckoning Jennie to follow her into some dark woodland that felt both inviting and malevolent. The deeper they would go, the more youthful her mother would become. Morphing back into the gorgeous songbird Jennie vividly recalled from her youth, way before her father's betrayal. Jennie would always call out to her, but she never stopped. Her mother would keep making her way into the dark. Then, suddenly, the thicket would open to reveal a small stone church in the middle of vast, endless rice fields. The church had a bell tower and she could see the bell moving, but she could never hear any sound.

'Take me home, Jennie,' she would hear her mother say before opening the wooden church door and disappearing from sight. In the dream, Jennie would run after her, but as soon as she opened the door, a thick, red wave of blood rushed out and washed her away. She would wake up choking and gagging on the faint taste of metallic iron in her mouth. At first, the dream came to her once a week, then two to three times. Then, one night after coming back late from another night of drinking and passing out, she nearly choked to death when she woke up mid-vomit. Even for Jennie, this was a first. By then, she was having the exact same dream almost every day. 'Okay mom,' she remembered saying eventually. 'You win. I guess, I'll take you home.'

As soon as she made the decision, she was immediately overcome with a sense of inexplicable clarity and peace. She picked up her guitar for the first time in months and actually wrote a song. Something she hadn't done since she'd had to look after her mom at the hospital. It felt good and she thought back to the time she had written a silly song about adopting a cat, hoping that she could convince her mother to let her keep one in their cramped one bedroom. It never did happen. But at least they had ended up having a memorable afternoon of singing and making up lyrics about an imaginary ginger and white cat that they had named Scrappy.

Soon after, Jennie began to make plans. Even if it just didn't make sense for her to return her mother's remains back to Albay. If not for the vivid dreams telling her otherwise, Jennie had thought that it would really not matter to her mom all that much. How could it? She had never even expressed any desire to return home or made any effort to visit or contact her grandparents even after Jennie was born. Why did she suddenly want her remains to be returned there? It confused and interested Jennie in equal measure.

At first, she was going to make the trip on her own when, all of a sudden, Brian announced that he was going to tag along too. He claimed that he wanted to make sure that she would come back to Hong Kong. Jennie, on the other hand, knew better. He just needed an excuse to get out of town and skip out on paying the money he owed to Digger—his cocaine dealer.

'You really should pay him, Bri! Doesn't he know where you live?' Jennie was legitimately worried for him.

'He KNOWS where my parents live! Ha!' he laughed it off.

The more Jennie thought about going to the Philippines with Brian, the better it sounded. She knew no one there; it could be weird. Or worse, it could be dangerous. It was best to go with someone who could look out for her. If he managed to stay sober long enough, that is.

'Do you think they'll have pot there? I mean, it's up in the boondocks, right?' Brian asked. Surprisingly, he had many valid questions about the trip and their destination. Many of which Jennie hadn't even considered before booking their flight tickets. The more he asked, the more she realized how little she knew of her mother's birthplace. Her mother had always made It-Ba sound like a rough and wild version of a rehab centre. Every time she would threaten to send Jennie over, she'd go on and on about how remote it is. How there's no electricity, no TVs, no phones, no bars, and worse, no drugs! Also, they apparently practise a very strict religion there. Her grandparents would make her pray—a lot!—and make her believe in the power of monsters, magic, and stuff. As if all of that would have scared her enough to get her on the road to sobriety. If only it were that easy.

'Bri, you know there may not be any access to anything at all, you realize that, right? Just because it's in the boondocks doesn't mean they grow pot there.'

They were having this conversation in the tiny room that she was renting in Kwun Tong. A place that had been paid for by her father who still thought that she was using the money as tuition for her first year at uni. She had dropped out without telling him. She figured that it was okay, since he didn't really care what she did with her life.

'It's cool if they don't!' Brian pronounced confidently, stretching his body across her futon, exposing a tattoo of a scrawled heart on his left hip. It looked like it had been drawn by child, when in fact, it had been drawn by an ex. 'I should probably detox anyway,' he added.

Jennie rolled her eyes at him. 'Whatever, just don't expect much, okay?'

She had never liked that tattoo. Not because it was drawn by an ex but because it annoyed Jennie how unbothered he was by something so ugly being on his body. How unbothered he was by anything at all actually. There was something about his easy-going nature that sometimes got on her nerves. Something about it reminded her about how wound up she felt most of the times. Maybe, one day, she'd get him to remove it.

'Expectations set at zero! Brian proclaimed. 'Although . . . we should probably see if we can pick something up when we land in Manila, yeah?'

Jennie and Brian didn't find any drugs, but they did get hammered. As soon as they landed in Manila, they ended up going for a few drinks in the red-light district in Makati. Just in case—they had agreed between themselves—they couldn't get any drinks in It-Ba. The two ended up drinking until 5 a.m., got their phones stolen, and subsequently, nearly missed their domestic flight the following day.

They arrived in Albay, hungover, hungry, and in serious need of assistance. When their ride dropped them off in the municipality of Manito, supposedly the last main town before It-Ba, they discovered that none of the tricycle drivers knew of or had even heard of It-Ba. At first, Jennie assumed that it was all due to miscommunication. Maybe they weren't pronouncing the name correctly? It would have helped if they had their mobile phones with them and could point to where this town was on a map. But the more they insisted on its existence, the more confused looks they got from the locals, which, combined with the hangover, made them even more frustrated. The more frustrated they became, the more aggravated they acted until, eventually, no one by the tricycle stand wanted to be anywhere near them. So, when Samael turned up just as they were ready to give up, they thought he was a godsend.

'It-Ba? You need to go to It-Ba?' Samael had appeared seemingly out of nowhere.

Jennie almost jumped up to hug him. 'Ohmygad, yes! You know It-Ba?'

'Yes, I know. I can take you there!' He smiled. 'I'm Samael,' he extended his hand, but Brian hugged him instead. 'You are a lifesaver, dude!' he exclaimed, as if he had just found a long-lost friend.

'My tricycle is on the other side, though. Are you okay to walk over?' He motioned towards their luggage. 'Let me help,' he said and flashed Jennie a sweet smile. It made her blush a little.

'So, how come those guys over there don't know where this town is?' Brian asked as they began to make their way to the tricycle.

Samael shook his head. 'Oh, its' cause most of those guys aren't really from around here.'

'But where are they from then?' Jennie was confused.

'Not from Albay and definitely not from Manito. A lot of people from other towns like Sorsogon or Camarines come over to make a living here, since there are more tourists,' he said. 'Make more money,' he added with a wink. She was beginning to like him.

'Are you from here, Samael? Or are you actually from It-Ba?' Jennie asked, excited to finally meet someone from her mother's mysterious hometown.

'I'm not from It-Ba, but I've lived here my whole life! I know everything about Albay. If you need help with anything, I'm your guy!'

Jennie wasn't really surprised by what came out of Brian's mouth next. 'I'm so glad to hear that! Do you know where we can get some pot?'

Samael's face brightened even more, 'After I take you to It-Ba, I'll get you some myself. It's from my own farm.'

Brian thew Jennie an excited look and almost squealed with delight. 'Oh man, this trip just got better!'

'Yeah, this trip has definitely improved,' she said, smiling widely now. Jennie thought back to what her mom had said about having no drugs in It-Ba. Had she been lying? Or had things changed that much since she'd left home? Minutes later, they were standing next to Samael's tricycle. It looked cozy enough for three people but for three people and two large backpacks? Jennie could only hope that the drive to It-Ba wouldn't take too long.

'By the way, you guys must be thirsty . . .' Samael reached for bottles of water inside a blue Styrofoam cooler at the front of his tricycle. 'Here,' he said as he handed a cold one to each of them.

'Ah mate!' Brian reached for the plastic bottle immediately and without hesitation, started emptying the contents into his mouth. Jennie did the same.

'We're so glad you found us!' Brian exclaimed and threw the empty bottle into a nearby bin.

Jennie felt instantly refreshed. 'Wow! Is this magic water?' she asked. Her hangover was becoming a faint memory surprisingly fast. 'I really needed that, thanks.'

Samael flashed her his easy-going smile again and said, 'You're welcome.'

Jennie watched him curiously as he proceeded to load their luggage at the back of his tricycle. *What is it about this guy?* she thought, trying to figure him out. Something about that handsome smile made it very easy to trust him. For a second, it made her feel uneasy, but then the feeling went away just as quickly as it came.

'Let's go to It-Ba!' Samael announced before he enthusiastically jumped on his tricycle.

They'd been on the road for almost an hour when the way unexpectedly got bumpier. By then, the landscape turned from buzzy, provincial small town to bucolic barangay huts to dense wilderness. Jennie revelled in breathing in the clean air. She hadn't realized how bad the air was in Hong Kong until then. It made her feel even better about taking her mom back. Why had she waited so long? She was suddenly annoyed with herself for being such a fuck-up. It made her crave a drink and a bump of coke or, in this case, light up a joint.

After a little while more, the tricycle stopped, and Samael offloaded their bags from the back. Jennie and Brian got out and looked at the rough path ahead of them. There was nothing but a rugged trail of rocks disappearing into a thicket of trees.

'This can't be it, can it?' Brian asked, looking around at the quiet and empty woodland surrounding them.

'No, not yet,' Samael said and began to walk in the direction where the rocky path ended. Jennie noticed that he was carrying her backpack on his back.

'I can carry that for you,' Samael motioned to her nylon hand carry.

'Oh no!' Jennie held her bag to her chest. 'It's okay. I can carry this one, thank you!'

She opened the top of her bag to get a quick peek at the wooden Chinese box that held her mother's ashes. The ornately carved Chinese box had been a gift from one of her mom's fans in Hong Kong. A male admirer with money— one of the many relationship opportunities she had turned down to stay with her father. It used to contain some of her favourite costume jewellery, now it contained her remains. *Nearly there, Ma,* Jennie thought to herself.

'Okay, from here,' Samael announced, 'we walk to It-Ba.' He said it like it was no problem at all.

Jennie and Brian groaned. 'Really? Is it still far from here?' Jennie asked. She could feel her headache coming back.

'It's not far, don't worry. Let's go.' Samael quickly disappeared through the trees.

Jennie was the first one to follow him in. 'Hey, wait!' she called after him.

'But what about your tricycle? You're just going to leave it here?' Brian wondered out loud. When he realized that he'd been left alone on the road, he quickly chased after them.

'The trike will be fine. Everyone here knows it's mine,' Samael yelled back and kept walking forward.

Brian walked up to Jennie and placed his arms over her shoulders. 'You still think this is a good idea?' he asked, half joking. Jennie shook her head. 'I just realized we blindly trusted a complete stranger who is now walking ahead of us with my stuff. We might be idiots.'

Brian laughed. *There he is again with that easy going attitude*, Jennie thought. It annoyed her that they were not being careful enough. They'd already lost their phones, so she figured they should at least try and be more careful about the rest of their belongings.

Suddenly, Samael stopped and waited for both of them to catch up to him.

'I'm here to help you, not steal your stuff,' he said good-naturedly. Jennie and Brian looked at each other in disbelief and felt somewhat embarrassed. *How could he have heard us?* Jennie thought to herself.

'Uh, no disrespect meant dude, we appreciate the help really,' Brian said and adjusted his backpack. They'd only been walking a few minutes, but his shirt was already drenched. Jennie suspected he was having the coke sweats. 'By the way, how come your English is so good man?' he asked, changing the topic. 'Is everyone's English in this place as good as yours?'

'YouTube,' Samael replied. 'I watch a lot of YouTube videos.'

Jennie and Brian looked at him with knotted eyebrows, trying to figure out if he was being serious. Samael started to laugh. 'You don't believe me? It really helps.'

Brian turned to Jennie. 'Well, hey, they have internet here if there's YouTube.'

'Yeah, except now we don't have our phones with us, do we?'

'The internet is better near Manito. In It-Ba, it's not so good,' Samael warned.

Jennie shrugged. 'Just as well.'

Samael turned to walk again and the two followed him deeper into the woods.

'By the way,' Samael started, 'what brings you both to It-Ba? Not a lot of tourists come to this area at all.'

Jennie thought of her mom's ashes in her bag. 'Oh, uh, I'm visiting my mother's family.'

'Who? I know almost everyone in It-Ba! What's your mother's name?' Samael was almost excited.

For a panicked second, Jennie could not recall her mother's name. She looked at him dumbfounded and embarrassed. 'It's uhhhh . . .'

Even Brian gave her a look that clearly said, *What the fuck Jennie?*

It came to her almost like a whisper. 'Severina,' she managed to finally say out loud.

'Her name was Sevvie Palomo . . . well Severina.'

Samael thought for a second. 'I don't really know any Palomos in It-Ba.'

'Oh, actually . . . Palomo is my dad's . . . her maiden name is Vargas.'

'Vargas! You're related to the balyana,' Samael exclaimed.

Jennie didn't know what a balyana was but what piqued her interest more was that he actually knew her mother's family. 'You know them?'

'Everyone knows the family of the balyana! They will be so happy to see you.'

'Great! But what's a balyana?' Jennie finally managed to ask.

His answer confused and surprised her. 'A priest,' he said.

Just then, they stepped into a clearing and the landscape instantly opened up to a vast rice field. Beyond it were rows of stone and wooden huts jutting from the horizon. They had arrived in It-Ba.

'We're here!' Samael announced.

Jennie and Brian could not believe their eyes. Just seconds ago, it had seemed like they were surrounded by nothing but tall trees and now, unbelievably, they'd suddenly arrived.

'Oh wow!' Jennie was in awe as she surveyed the pastoral landscape in front of her. She heard Brian exclaim something like, 'Cool!' before Samael's voice beckoned them to follow him once more. That's when she spotted it. The church in the middle of a rice field, just like in her dreams. She stopped to look, transfixed by the glimmering stones that made up the mostly black structure. She had never noticed the colour in her dreams before. Suddenly, she was gripped by a sense of foreboding.

'Jennie, come on!' She heard Brian call out to her.

She was about to turn around when she noticed the cat. It was white and ginger with black, round eyes that seemed to recognize her. It was standing at the edge of the church steps in front of the wooden door—like one of the stone lions in front of the HSBC tower on Queen's Road. Then, as if to say, 'Go on, follow your friends,' it lifted its pink nose at her and disappeared into the rice fields. She turned back towards Brian and Samael and ran after them.

'We'll have to go around the back, okay?' Samael turned to them, sounding unexpectedly cautious. 'I'm avoiding some people in town.'

'Why, because you're a local celebrity?' Brian joked.

Samael laughed. 'Something like that.'

He led them through narrow paths alongside well-constructed houses of bamboo and stone. Jennie observed that most homes had colourful wooden fencing and well-kept lawns filled with jewel-toned, vivid flowers. She found herself charmed by it all. Had they somehow stumbled into an unknown Philippine version of the Shire from *The Lord of the Rings*? But then she also noticed the emptiness. *Where was everyone?*

Finally, after going around a few more houses, Samael stopped in front of the biggest house in the area. A mansion compared to the other houses. To Jennie, it felt similar to the church in the fields. Except it had ornate wooden doors and windows. The path to the house was lined with verdant blooming rainbow hued flowers planted in big red pots. There was even a rattan swing on the stone porch.

Brian took the words right out of her mouth when he said, 'Oh damn, is this where your family lives Jennie? It's amazing!'

'Tao po!' Samael called out, entering the house without even knocking.

'Hey, shouldn't we . . .' she started, worried that they were imposing on whoever lived there.

Just then, an old man in woman's clothing appeared around the corner.

'Po-on?' he called out.

'Samael po!' Samael quickly corrected him.

For a second, Jennie thought the man was going to bow down in front of Samael, but Samael caught one of his outstretched hands and placed it on his forehead instead.

A sign of respect for old people that Jennie was very familiar with. The old man, however, seemed very confused.

'*May bisita po kayo*, Manoy boy!'[2] Samael said immediately and gestured toward the couple.

Jennie immediately felt very self-conscious, but Brian coolly stepped forward and grabbed the old man's left hand. Then, without missing a beat, he placed it on his forehead, just as Samael had.

'Hi, I'm Brian!' he said. The whole scene unexpectedly made Jennie giggle.

'Severina,' the old man said, addressing her suddenly. Jennie froze at the sound of his voice. It was deep and surprisingly arresting for someone who looked like a hipster granny. He was wearing a patchwork quilt robe over a long skirt and his greying hair was tied up in a neat bun. The old man didn't just walk over to her, he swanned over. She thought there was something almost unreal and comical about the way he carried himself. Like an old-world movie star or a beauty pageant contestant. When he got closer, she noticed he was also wearing some light eye make-up. The way he eyed her intently reminded Jennie of the way her mother used to look at her when she had done something really bad. It made her feel nervous.

'No, I'm . . . mother ko po is Severina.[3] How did you know?' she stammered.

The old man took her hands and held them close to his chest. '*Anong ngaran mo, anak?*'[4] he asked.

'Jennie. *Ako po si* Jennie.'[5]

---

2 'You have a visitor, Manoy boy!'
3 '. . . my mother is Severina.'
4 'What is your name, child?'
5 'I am Jennie.'

'*Sain an nanay mo? Sain si* Severina, Jennie?'[6]

Jennie didn't speak much Tagalog but she understood well enough. The Bicolano dialect, however, was tricky for her. But what concerned her more than anything in that moment was revealing to this strange old man who clearly knew her mother that Severina had passed away. She debated if taking out the box with her mother's ashes would be the right thing to do.

'Are you related to my mother? *Kamag-anak ko po ba kayo?*'[7]

He smiled at her '*Anak ko si* Severina, *iha*.[8] I'm your grandfather.'

He pulled her in, and they hugged. He was still holding her when more people came into the room. There was an older woman, possibly her grandmother. Then, a teenage boy came in with a little girl in tow. They first noticed Samael and seemed excited by his unexpected presence. Jennie could tell he was motioning for them to not make a fuss and tried directing their attention to her and her grandfather instead.

'*Andito po ang apo nyo galing ng* Hong Kong Manay Mher! *Si* Jennie *po at si* Brian, *kasama nya*,'[9] Samael said to the old woman.

The kids, meanwhile, walked over to Samael to kiss his hand. *That's odd*, Jennie thought. She couldn't decide if it reminded her of the Don Corleone scene from *The Godfather* or the way Christians would go up to religious figures to show devotion. Either way, it distracted somewhat from the uncomfortable reunion she was experiencing in the moment.

---

[6] 'Where is your mother? Where is Severina, Jennie?'

[7] 'Are you related to me?'

[8] 'Oh, Severina is my daughter.'

[9] 'Your grandson from Hong Kong Manay Mher is here! Jennie and Brian, with him.'

Even Brian was quiet. He just stood there, watching everything with a big goofy expression on his face. She suddenly wished he would do something stupid to break the awkwardness.

Eventually, her grandfather let go and he called on the rest of the family.

'*Andito na ang anak ni* Severina!¹⁰ She's home,' he said out loud. Nieces, nephews, uncles, and aunts came out from different areas of the house to meet her. Jennie began to wonder if the whole Vargas clan lived there. In an instant, she went from being a single child and knowing only her father and mother to becoming a part of bigger family. It was overwhelming and comforting at the same time. She wasn't alone after all. By the time all the family introductions were done, Jennie noticed that Samael had gone.

'*May pinuntahan lang si* Samael, *iha*.¹¹ He said he will return,' her grandfather, Manoy Boy, said after she started looking for him. All Jennie could think of, however, was the weed that he had promised them.

'*Bago ang lahat* Jennie . . . *kwento mo naman sa amin and buhay nyo ni* Severina *sa* Hong Kong.¹² How did she die?'

Jennie looked at him wide eyed and asked, 'How do you know that she died? Who told you?'

Jennie couldn't figure out why, but his response to her question sent a chill down her spine. '*Wala namang nag-kwento sa akin*.¹³ I know, because you're here.'

---

¹⁰ 'Severina's child is here!'

¹¹ 'Samael just went to see someone.'

¹² 'We don't know anything about you Jennie . . . tell us about your life with Severina in Hong Kong.'

¹³ 'No one told me anything.'

She spent the rest of the day catching up with her grandparents while Brian passed out in the guest room the family had prepared for them. Jennie had so many questions herself, but both her grandparents were desperate to know more about her mother instead. She told them everything. The good, the bad, and the ugly. It was the first time she'd spoken to anyone about what really happened to her mother. Afterwards, it felt as if a great weight had been lifted off her chest. She felt relieved—and oddly—cleansed. Like she'd been absolved of all her sins

Her grandparents insisted that they stay for a few days, even weeks. They had planned to spend just a night, maybe two, in It-Ba and then go to a bigger town to see if they could get a temporary mobile phone before moving somewhere near a beach. But Jennie couldn't really say no them. Especially after how emotional they had become at the sight of her mother's ashes in the box. *A few days wouldn't hurt,* she thought. They could decompress, figure out what to do next, and get to know her family more. There was also the matter of the gathering or the fiesta, as her grandfather put it. As luck would have it, Brian and Jennie had arrived at the beginning of It-Ba's most revered religious festival. The Halia—five days of feasting, drinking, and dancing in celebration of the full moon to honour the town's patron saint. Jennie and Brian could never say no to a party and what a rager it turned out to be.

It was a struggle, but Jennie eventually managed to flush the carnage of vomit down the toilet. The whole time she thought how much easier (and much less disgusting) it would

have been if she could have just pushed a button to make it all disappear. Now, if she could just have a bottle of Pocari Sweat and two Advils, she'd be better. It was the first time since she arrived in town that she actually missed Western conveniences. Who would have thought that a party in the boondocks could be so wild?

But just like every other time she's had a crazy night, she was a little fuzzy on most of the details. Not because she didn't remember what happened. On the contrary, everything was clear in her mind, it was just . . . she couldn't tell which memory was real and which a weed-induced fever dream. Thinking back to Samael's gift last night made her want to light up again. If there was any reason that would make her stay longer, despite the non-flushing toilets, this would be it. She would stay if it meant she could smoke as much as she could of that herb. The high was sublime happiness, a spiritual transcendence she never experienced before. If only she could take some back with her to Hong Kong. Something she was sure Brian had already started to try and figure out. She'd have to talk to him about it as soon as she saw him.

Regardless of Samael's herb, It-Ba revealed itself to Jennie last night. She remembered that as soon as the sun went the down, the whole town came alive, and its inhabitants came out of the woodwork. Every home was lit up with colourful lanterns, every home had a feast prepared. Then, there was live music provided by a raucous roving band, that had people dancing and singing on the street. It was a loud and festive celebration that started from her grandfather's home. She recalled that as soon as she came out of the guest room with Brian to join the festivities, her grandfather had two glasses of a coconut liqueur cocktail ready for them. Neither of them had ever had anything as good before. Nor anything as potent.

Unsurprisingly, this was when, she recalled, things began to feel really off kilter.

'*Especial* recipe *ko yan*,'[14] he winked at them with bedazzled lashes.

Jennie didn't think he could be any more flamboyant than when she first saw him, but she was delightfully surprised. He was wearing a full face of make-up, and his long, greying hair tumbled in big bouncy curls down to his waist. In place of his patchwork robe, he wore an extravagant black robe with ornate red and gold details. *He only needs a pointy hat*, Jennie thought, *and he'd look like a wizard. A cross-dressing wizard.*

'Oh, *muntik ko nang makalimutan!*'[15] He suddenly exclaimed and reached for a small, native pouch inside his robe. He handed it to Jennie. 'Samael said this is for both of you.'

Jennie's eyes widened when she opened the pouch. It contained dried, loose, fragrant leaves, a wad of rolling papers, and a small box of matches. Brian actually whooped with joy.

'Samael grows the best.' Manoy Boy addressed Brian, 'I think you will like very much.'

'Oh wow, do you mind if we roll some now?' Brian was trying to contain his excitement but wasn't doing a good job

---

[14] 'That's my special recipe'
[15] 'Oh, I almost forgot!'

of it. Jennie thought it was adorable that he was still trying to be polite when all they talked about earlier was smoking the pot Samael promised them.

Manoy Boy giggled. 'Go ahead! I've already had one.'

'*Saan po si* Samael, Manoy?[16] Will he be joining the fiesta?' Manoy Boy had insisted earlier that she call him Manoy Boy instead of Lolo.

'*Mamaya daw sya babalik.*[17] He said you two should enjoy the celebrations.'

By the time her grandfather excused himself to meet visitors arriving at the door, Brian had already finished rolling one joint. He took the first hit.

'Goddamn!' he exclaimed and handed it to Jennie. As soon as she took a drag, everything changed. The immediate effect surprised her first. Jennie had never taken anything that worked so fast. At least nothing that was pot. It was like stepping into an alternate void. Everything seemed cocooned in this ethereal and glimmering, multi-coloured light that began to pulse. As it did, it began to talk to her. It told her that the Light was everything now and she should surrender to it completely.

She looked at Brian who stood next to her with the goofiest grin she'd even seen on anyone. Moments later, her grandfather would find them hugging each other, overwhelmed with love and inexplicable happiness. They were giggling like children while weeping at the same time.

'You are ready,' Manoy Boy said and smiled at both of them like a proud parent would.

---

[16] 'Where is Samael, Manoy?'

[17] 'He said he will come back later.'

Jennie turned to her grandfather and watched the Light create a halo around his figure. 'Ready, yes.' Jennie wasn't sure what exactly she was ready for but right now, she didn't care. She was the happiest she'd ever been, and the Light was telling her to do whatever her grandfather told her. Especially now that he was wearing a black pointy hat. Of course, she must follow this wizard.

When Jennie and Brian walked out to the front of the house, they discovered that the whole town had been waiting for them. As soon as they emerged, everyone erupted in joyous cheers. The band struck up a tune and people came up to place garlands of white flowers around their necks. They began to feel like royalty, but it wasn't until her grandfather motioned for them to take their seats on two rattan chairs placed like thrones on the front porch that they began to actually feel like a king and a queen. The chairs were on top of a platform with bamboo poles on each side, making it a mini podium that people could carry around.

Her grandfather addressed the excited crowd in Bicolano. Normally, Jennie would struggle to understand, but this time, she had the Light to make her understand. She watched it swirl around him as he spoke. 'Through the grace of our lord,' he beamed, 'we have been blessed with the homecoming of one of our own. We honour the death of my daughter, Severina, but we also celebrate the arrival of her daughter Jennie and her friend Brian, the curse breaker! Praise be.'

The crowd cheered at the mention of their names. Then, without warning, their podium thrones were lifted and carried by the crowd out of her grandfather's house and into the street. Brian began to laugh and clap his hands with glee. Jennie turned to him and was overwhelmed with inexplicable gratitude. *Her curse breaker.* She didn't know what it meant, but the Light said not to worry so she didn't.

They stopped at every house in It-Ba. Each time they did, people would have them drink the same coconut drink her grandfather had made for them earlier and smoke the same weed that Samael had left them. They would be offered food and sometimes some even offered jewellery while others gave them carved wooden figures of a terrifying winged creature. Most of them, Jennie observed, were given with such gratitude and joy that she had to ask her grandfather. 'Why are they doing this? We haven't done anything to deserve this.'

'Because, Jennie, you're saving them,' he said. Jennie noticed that the Light around him was pulsing even brighter.

'How?'

'Because of your gift to the Halia, no one from It-Ba will be offered to the Lord Asuang tonight.'

Jennie giggled, not fully comprehending what Manoy Boy had just said. 'What?'

'Has your mother told you about aswangs, Jennie?'

Jennie shook her head.

'They are powerful divine beings who assume a human form and walk the earth. They've existed before all of us were here. Before It-Ba, maybe even, before Mt Mayon.'

Manoy Boy nodded towards one of the many wooden winged figurines laid at her feet.

'One of them is our Lord Asuang, the creator and protector of It-Ba. He keeps us safe from outside danger, from sickness and pestilence. Because of him, we always have a good harvest. Because of him, no one goes hungry. He's responsible for all the beauty you see here in

It-Ba, all the goodness, all of it comes through the blessing of our Lord.'

Jennie stared closely at the wooden figures. All of them were of a creature that was half man, half beast. She thought all of them bore a close resemblance to Samael.

'The only thing he asks in return is a full moon blood offering.'

The Light moved to swirl around the wooden figures and Jennie remained mesmerized.

'Your mother was supposed to come back with an offering when she left all those years ago. But . . . well, you know what happened. Her misfortune . . . her death, is the result of a curse that falls on anyone who walks out on their sacred duty. This curse, Jennie, would have passed on to you if you had not come home. And now, with Brian here . . . we can break it.'

They both turned to Brian, who at that moment was taking another drag from a joint someone had rolled for him. *He's in heaven*, she thought.

'What's a blood sacrifice, Manoy?' she asked.

'Don't you worry about that now. First, we make an offering to break the curse. Then, we prepare you to become the next balyana! Like me.' He beamed.

Jennie knew that everything her grandfather had just said was evil and terrifying. She should have been screaming. She should have grabbed Brian's hand right then and there and run as far away as their feet could take them. But the Light was telling her that everything was okay. There was nothing to be afraid of. So, when her grandfather detailed to her what was going to happen later, she smiled and held Brian's hand.

She didn't even realize that tears had started streaming down her face until Brian wiped them away.

'Isn't this amazing?!' he exclaimed to her.

After a few more houses, the fanfare and the parade eventually moved to the rice fields. She heard the church bell ringing even before it came into view. In the darkness, the volcanic rocks that made up the structure glimmered like black diamonds. Jennie watched the Light make its way from the incoming crowd to the church where it lit every gas lamp and candle until the room glowed with warm, yellow rays. The procession continued its merrymaking until it reached the church steps and by the time Brian and Jennie stepped off their rattan thrones, everyone had fallen silent. Even the church bell stopped tolling.

'What happened to the music?' Brian slurred. Jennie could see that he could barely stand. Neither could she, but at least she had her grandfather and grandmother holding her up. They guided her to the front of the church as if she was about to get married. Then, as the townspeople began to file in and take their seats, Brian decided to start dancing in the middle aisle. She could hear him trying to get people to join him, but no one was in the mood to continue the party any more. Jennie would have likely joined him if she hadn't noticed the ginger and white cat.

'Oh look! it's Scrappy!' she exclaimed, remembering the cat song she made up with her mom all those years ago. Both her grandparents ignored her excitement and sat her down— almost impatiently—in the front. The cat was standing on the edge of a large, black marble table at the altar. As if it had been waiting for her all this time.

She watched it leap down from the table and jump into her lap. She wasn't event surprised when it spoke to her. 'I'm so sorry Jennie,' the cat said without opening its mouth. In Jennie's mind, it sounded just like her mother.

'Oh Ma, it's okay! The Light says everything will be okay.' She started petting it, oblivious to her grandfather who had started to lead the congregation in a prayer from behind the marble table. The townspeople responded back with chants of increasing passion. In the middle of it all, Brian continued to dance and sway.

'Don't tell anyone you can hear me, okay? This is our secret. I will help you get out of here. But first, we must break this curse,' her mother, the cat, said to her.

Jennie nodded, 'Okay Ma, I miss you!' she said and lovingly pressed the cat close to her chest. All of a sudden, the whole room erupted in a chorus.

'Si Asuang! Si Asuang! Si Asuanngggggg!'

It was immediately followed by a huge gust of wind. It swept through the church with inhuman ferocity, extinguishing all the candles and gas lamps inside. In the dark, Jennie began to sense a malignant force prowling around. It crept up and down the aisle, moving along on the stone floor with a chilling, clickity clack sound that made her picture giant claws. When it stopped, she heard the sound of tearing flesh and breaking bone. For a while it was the only sound she could hear. No one screamed and no one ran away. Even the cat stayed silent. Eventually, the horrific sound of dismemberment ended, followed by sickening thud. She felt another powerful surge of wind, but this time, it seemed to suck the air right out of the room.

Her grandfather was the first one to light one of the gas lamps. Jennie could see the relief on his face when he lifted it high above him. He stood behind the marble table, unfazed by the mangled carcass of a human being that was now splayed on top of it. There were streaks of blood everywhere, but instead of horror, the congregation erupted in cheers.

'The curse is broken, and the feast can now begin!' her grandfather announced. 'As the bearer of this sacrifice, we offer the first cut to Jennie.'

She watched her grandfather pull out a small knife to slice a piece of skin from the mutilated body. Jennie didn't remember much after that. The last thing she could recall was watching the cat jump down from her lap and lick the pool of blood off the floor.

Jennie stumbled out of the washroom and, in an instant, her head began to the throb. Between the alcohol, the weed, and the deranged visions of blood and talking cats, and trying to remember what happened last night, she was beginning to have a monster of a headache. She needed water. A lot of water.

She made her way towards her bed and immediately noticed a tall, clear jar of water and an empty glass. *My grandparents must have placed it there*, she thought and poured herself a tall drink. Then, as soon as she felt mildly better, she began to wonder about Brian. She couldn't tell if he had slept on his side of the bed or not. Although, from what she remembered of his condition last night, she wouldn't be surprised if he was passed out somewhere. It was not unlike him at all to stay wherever he found himself to sleep off his hangover. He was probably inside the church, she concluded, where she last remembered him dancing like an idiot.

She wanted to talk to him badly. She needed someone else to tell her how crazy real it all seemed and laugh about it. Jennie crept back into bed and was about to crawl under the sheets again when she found the cat curled up among the pillows.

'Scrappy?' She sat up and immediately noticed the streaks of red across its ginger and white fur. When she pulled the sheets off, she discovered red paw stains all over the sheets. A shiver ran through her, and she pushed the cat over the side of the bed. It landed on all fours on the floor where it began to lick itself. Jennie thought back to the images from the church last night and she broke out in a cold sweat. The wind, the blood streaks, the mutilated body on the marble slab. Then her grandfather offering her a piece of skin from the carcass.

She felt like throwing up again. Jennie was about to run back to the toilet when she noticed the cat eating something off the floor.

'Hey, no! What are you doing?' She nudged it off with her foot and it slinked away with an unhappy meow. When she saw the piece of human skin on the floor, it took her a minute to realize that she was looking at what she had vomited earlier. She remembered her grandfather's words.

'We offer you the first cut.'

She instantly fell to her knees. 'No, no, no.' Jennie began to shake as she struggled to accept the truth.

It wasn't until the cat came back to lick the skin clean that she noticed it had a portion of a badly scrawled heart tattoo on it.

That's when Jennie began to scream. She screamed with such fury that all of It-Ba heard her.

The Nurse

United Kingdom and Philippines

The sight of her made his blood run cold. That's how he could tell it was the same woman. He had first noticed her when they reached Daet—the third stop of a twelve-hour overnight bus he was on with his girlfriend Genie from Cubao to Legazpi City.

The woman appeared at hour eight.

Miguel felt her even before he saw her. Her gaze locked with his like the curled talons of some winged creature. He felt hooked, inexplicably compelled to look in her direction. The aberrant woman was sitting on a wooden bench for smoking customers outside Nana Tellie's roadside restaurant. At first glance she looked like any other bus passenger on their way home. Except, there was something eerily still about her, something that felt deceptive, something that didn't feel human. The thought made him feel ill at ease. Even from a distance, he could tell her gaze was fixed on him. But when he turned to look, all he could make out of was a blurry female figure. Miguel squinted his eyes, looked again and watched her fuzzy form stand and walk inside the restaurant. A shiver ran through his skin once more. *Odd*, he thought. Everything else around her, he could see clear as day. He blamed his poor eyesight on exhaustion but then he heard a voice in his head.

'*Remember me.*'

He remembered Genie, shivering and sick inside the bus. *I don't have time for this*, he decided. He reasoned away the strange encounter to lack of sleep and walked over to join the other passengers lining up to use the rest stop toilet.

Poor Genie.

Ever since they had landed back in Manila, her condition seemed to have gotten worse. Back in the UK, where they both worked as nurses, none of the doctors was able to diagnose what was wrong with her. She suffered from severe fatigue, unexplained body pain, weight loss, and lately, skin lesions. They had appeared on her left leg, first as a small patch of rash that, with time, grew into an angry cluster of red prickly bumps. It was impossible for Genie to resist the urge to pick at them. One night, after he had come back from the hospital, he found her in a confused state of relief and distress. She had been crying in frustration after another episode of furious scratching. When he had looked at her rashes, he was alarmed to discover that they had turned into open sores.

Alarmingly, there had been more. They had spread all over her left leg and started creeping on her shoulder and back, making it look like her skin was being consumed by fiery, smouldering lava.

'What is happening to me?' she had asked, weeping.

Miguel had never felt more helpless. He wished he could do something to make it stop. He wished this would happen to him instead. Not her. His beautiful, beloved Genie.

It pained him to see her this way. Helpless and sick. A reduced version of the vibrant girl he had met in Camalig not so long ago. He really hadn't been looking for anyone when their paths crossed, but there was something about her that made him think of the women back in olden times. A sweetness and purity, that, in his opinion, no longer existed. He was immediately smitten. They both loved being outdoors, climbing trees, and going for long walks. They hadn't been together long enough; true, but he knew then she was the one. He hadn't left her side since.

That night, he had made her bowl of chicken rice porridge for dinner with extra ginger, just as she liked. Then, he had soaked several hand towels in a cool medicated bath and placed them over her sores. She had fallen asleep in his arms while he softly whispered calming reassurances into her ear.

'I will take care of you. Don't worry, my love,' he had cooed with devoted tenderness.

Miguel had barely slept that night, but he didn't mind. He tended to her, making sure that the cold compress was applied fresh on her skin throughout the night. He wanted her to have a good night's sleep.

'*Remember . . .*' that voice in his head again.

The morning after her itching incident, he had taken the day off from work—again—to take her back to the doctor. They were prescribed a bag of pills and creams, none of which had worked. In fact, Miguel was convinced that they had only made her condition worse.

In the end, they had both taken too much time off work. So, it hadn't really been a surprise when the hospital served them their termination contracts. *Just as well*, Miguel had thought. London hadn't really been working out for them. Between the gruelling twelve-hour shifts and the not-so-casual racism they'd faced from doctors and patients, life had not been as ideal as they thought it would be. Besides, he was getting sick of the cold. He longed for warmth; he longed for the sun. Most of all, he longed for home.

'*Remember me . . .*' the voice persisted.

He was back in the bus now, standing on the aisle next to Genie with a hot cup of bone broth when—

'*Remember, Ado . . .*'

He looked up and turned to the window. She was hovering outside now, the blurry lady from the bench. Her form dark and jagged against the streaks of humidity on the plexiglass window. The sight of her was both so surprising and menacing that blood instantly drained away from his body.

It's her again, he thought. His skin broke out in goosebumps, confused by the cold pinpricks of unexplainable recognition washing over him. He stood in the bus aisle, paralysed, trying to make sense of what he was seeing and what he was hearing in his mind. He could hear her breathing, saying his name. The sound of her voice began to fill his mind and was getting progressively louder until it felt like she was about to come in through the window. But not for him, for her. For his beloved Genie.

'Excuse po,' said the teenager standing next to him.

He gasped in surprise, nearly spilling the broth on Genie.

'Excuse,' she repeated, a little louder this time. He turned to her, terrified but also relieved for the reminder that everything was still, well . . . normal.

He looked around. He was still inside the bus; the lights were off and the air-conditioning was on full artic blast as it had been since the trip started. The teenager ignored him and looked down at Genie instead.

'*Makiki-raan lang po,*'[18] the teenager said pointedly to Genie this time.

He looked at her, dumbstruck for a few seconds, before he realized that Genie had slipped off her chair. She was still asleep but her head and her arm was partially obstructing the aisle. The teen didn't even wait for him to do anything. She slipped past him and snuck sideways around Genie to get to her seat at the back of the bus. *How rude*, he thought before turning his attention back to the window with dread.

The woman was gone.

The tightness in his chest eased up immediately. But her voice, he could still hear it echoing in his mind. Reminding him about . . . something.

Miguel was immediately gripped with grave unease. Whoever this woman was, she clearly meant to do Genie harm. But why? And then a grimmer question: What was she? He gave Genie a gentle nudge to move her completely back to her seat and she turned to face the window with a restless moan.

---

[18] 'May I pass through, please?'

'Genie . . .' he whispered to her, 'I have bone broth here for you.'

She groaned, muttered a soft 'no', and then went quiet again. Just then, Miguel heard the bus driver close the door, and the engine start again. He took a sip of Genie's broth and carefully moved to take his seat next to her. Nervously, he watched the bus manoeuvre its way out of the eatery parking lot before finding its way to the main road. His anxiety only eased up slightly after the bus put more kilometres between him and that phantom woman. He turned to look at Genie and took added comfort in her oblivious, somnolent state. Suddenly, he thought back to a conversation he had overheard back in London.

Could it be?

It was perhaps the hardest phone call Genie had to make. Soon after getting their work contract terminated from the hospital, she called her mom. Through tears, she kept saying, 'I'm sorry,' as if losing the job had been her fault. She cried about the money she wouldn't be able to provide, she cried about the promises she wouldn't be able to keep, most of all, she cried hard about the money she still owed the agency that had placed her in London.

'I don't know what to do. Where am I going to get that money from, Ma?'

'Genie, that's not important now,' her mother assured her. 'Just come home soon. With God's mercy, we'll figure out what to do.'

Genie wailed harder. 'I don't know, Ma . . . I think God has abandoned me.'

'Ssshhhhh, Genie, don't say that!' her mom quickly admonished her.

But Genie continued to sob in heartbreaking despair. 'Then why is this happening to me?!'

'You shouldn't blame God for what's happening, Genie. This isn't God's work. This . . . this is something else,' Genie's mom said forcefully, as if she knew exactly what was causing Genie's condition.

'I have a feeling you're being haunted by a Maligno.'

Miguel didn't quite believe what he had heard. Maligno. Genie's mom was actually talking about being haunted by a Maligno. After having heard that, the rest of the conversation seemed so senseless and unbelievable that he lost some of the details. Something about coming home immediately so Genie could see the local witch doctor. A sacrifice of some sort would be required, prayers and incantations would be recited, and special oils and herbs would be used to exorcise the Maligno to prevent it from haunting Genie again.

'People still believe in that kind of thing?' he said to Genie after she got off the emotional phone call, careful not to sound too disapproving and add to her distress. But Genie was too emotionally drained to respond. She simply curled up in his arms and fallen asleep.

Back in the bus, Miguel strained to discern the shapes speeding past his foggy window as he began to consider the unimaginable.

The phantom woman. Was she the Maligno that was haunting his beloved right now? It would certainly explain what he had just experienced. But how? And why? After they had left to work in the UK, he thought they'd left such old-fashioned, superstitious beliefs back in Camalig. And for a while, they had. There simply had been no time to think about anything other than getting settled in that strange new country, where everything had been so foreign and far away from home that it was unfathomable for anything like a Maligno to take hold. Not only that, Genie was the kindest, gentlest, most considerate, and respectful person he'd ever known. He simply could not imagine anyone or anything wanting to cause her any harm. No, not his beautiful Genie. He struggled to make sense of what was happening and feared what the rest of the evening had in store for them.

Whoever or whatever this creature was, Miguel sensed that the encounter at the eatery wouldn't be the last. He knew this even as he denied the existence of Malignos.

He pressed his hand against the window to wipe off the condensation rolling down the glass. He suddenly felt annoyed with himself for giving this whole ridiculous situation too much thought. Miguel tried to get his mind off it by trying to focus on what was real instead.

He looked out at the road, fixing his eyes on the different shuttered houses along the way. Just then, another overnight bus passed them by. Miguel watched it make its way to the front, observing the sleeping passengers from the window as it passed by. Miguel thought about their journey. Were they all going home? Would it be a joyful homecoming? He was struck by the normalcy of it all. *This is what's real,* he thought. It was crazy to think that Maligno's exist. *Because . . .* he searched his thoughts, *they don't!* He sighed audibly. Genie stirred next to him.

Miguel caressed her cheek and adjusted the blanket covering her, making sure that she was fully covered and warm. It was freezing inside the bus, but the cold didn't really bother him as much as it did her or anyone else for that matter. It made Miguel smile. Perhaps the harsh winters in the UK had conditioned him to finally get used to cold weather.

'*Remember me . . .*'

Her voice again. It sounded more distinct this time. More urgent.

He looked out the window and saw her standing rigidly across the road. Her eyes fixed on his for mere seconds before the bus sped past where she was standing. This time, he could see her clear as day, her form revealed in the moonlight. Miguel sank deeper into his seat, terrified. He shut his eyes and desperately tried to remove the image of her from his mind.

Instead, he only saw her more vividly and she was . . .

a beauty.

She reminded him of a forest nymph—the way her long, black hair framed her luminous, elfin face. It flowed down to her slender waist and seemed to move with the fluidity of water.

'*Ado . . . remember now.*'

But her true beauty lay in her eyes. It reached deep inside him. An almond-shaped passage, lined deep with verdant roots, bark, and foliage. A lush forest that called to him, asking him to come home.

No.

'No,' he repeated out loud and opened his eyes. Miguel looked around to see if anyone had noticed his distress, but no one moved. Not even Genie, who remained crumpled next to him, fast asleep.

'I won't let her harm you, Genie, I swear!' he whispered to her in panic, even though he had no idea just how he was going to do that. Despite what this creature had shown him in his mind, somehow, he knew with certainty that it was evil.

'*Ado . . . I will make you remember.*'

The woman's face was right next to the window. Miguel's skin bristled with horror, and he screamed. She pressed her face against the glass. Her nose and lips squeezed through the window inch by inch as the rest of her body floated alongside the bus, unfurling like black tendrils of foul smoke. It crept up thick and fast to join the rest of her body until she was intangible enough to press her form in.

Once inside the bus, she hovered like a menacing angel above Miguel who continued to scream with frightening, hysterical intensity.

He threw his body on top of Genie and yelled, 'You will not hurt her! Leave us alone!'

Genie fitfully squirmed, broke from under his hold and turned to the aisle. She continued to sleep while the rest of the passengers stirred quietly under their jackets and blankets. A cough was heard from the front and someone was snoring loudly in the back.

In spite of all the noise he was making, all the passengers were undisturbed by Miguel's screams of terror. Eventually, the phantom woman settled her dark ethereal form along the aisle, right next to Genie's seat.

'*Stop it, Ado. This is no longer amusing,*' she said to him without moving her lips. Her voice was warm and familiar inside his head.

Miguel's scream dwindled to a squeak and crumpled in his throat. He stood up and looked around the bus. It was a trick. She had them all in some kind of a spell, he reasoned in his mind as his eyes darted around, looking for someone who could tell him what was really happening right now. There was only the persistent hum of the air conditioner as the bus swerved left to follow the curve of the road ahead. He turned to her, baffled and curious at the same time.

'Who are you?' he demanded 'What do you want from us?!'

'*You know who I am,*' she said in a tone that verged on impatience. '*And while I may have everyone on this bus under my spell . . .*

you, however,' she added, looking down at Genie, '*have this one deep under yours.*'

Instinctively, Miguel held his left hand up to prevent her from getting any closer while his other hand landed protectively on Genie. Her reaction to what he did was nothing like he could have ever imagined.

Her face darkened and tears started running down her ghostly cheeks.

'*You're breaking my heart, Ado,*' she said. Her tone was strikingly more wounded than how it had sounded in his mind before. It was almost as if he was talking to a completely different being now, not a terrifying phantom woman but just a girl—a girl in pain, and somehow, he was the reason.

'Please stop calling me Ado. My name's not Ado, it's Miguel.'

He watched the tears continue to flow down her face in beaded droplets. Her weeping made him think of how it rained in a forest—a forest he'd been to before. For a second, he could even smell the trees.

'*No, you are Ado. I am Ada,*' she said, her lips quivering from the hurt he could still not grasp. '*We are one . . . bound by the spiritual forebearers that breathed life into the land you are now travelling through. The land that is our home.*'

And then he saw it. A pristine stream flowing into a river that rushed through a great, big forest that no human eye could perceive. He saw Genie walking through, enthralled by the glittering rolling water that led her there.

'*She wandered in uninvited into our home, Ado. Our laws dictate that she be punished for her transgression.*'

Ado watched Genie in his mind, walking through towering rows of coconut and abaca trees. Completely unaware that she had somehow broken through the imperceptible barrier separating the real from the otherworldly—an abundant green paradise populated by ancient spirits that lived in the soil, water, and air. Some call them Elementals but the locals refer to them as Engkantos. They've quietly co-existed with humans since he can remember but only because they abide by strict laws that guarantee the survival of their realm. In their world, no human can ever come through without permission and no human can ever leave without paying the price of trespassing.

'*You were only meant to make her suffer Ado, not fall in love with her.*'

He looked down at Genie still asleep in her seat and began to see things as they really were. His fingers passed through her, and he discovered that he was just as ghostly as Ada. Moments of their life together in the UK rushed through his head and he found himself unseen. A ghost, nothing but a malevolent spectre clinging to Genie's humanity. The revelation started to tighten around his heart, and he began to panic.

'No, no . . .' He looked at Ada, at the anguish tearing her up inside.

'But . . . I am Miguel . . . I lived in London as a nurse . . .' he faltered, struggling to remember his life now—his borrowed life, 'a registered . . . nurse . . .'

This is her life not yours, Ado. You took it as your own the longer you stayed with her. It was the only way for you to survive, having lived so far away from our world after her incursion. She became your only connection to our land . . .

'But I took care of her . . . I looked after her.'

'She looked after herself. You merely attached yourself to her life force, draining it away.'

'I love her.'

'This is why she's suffering, Ado. Your love'—Ada paused in disgust—*'it's making her sick. It's killing her.'*

Genie moaned in discomfort as the truth finally settled and sank in Miguel's mind. Ada was right, he was killing her. His kind inherently rejected humans. Her sickness, the skin lesions—it was his elemental nature attacking her corporeal form. He realized now that as soon as she got home to her family, she would be taken to the *albularyo* and he would be exorcised from her life. A ritual that would most likely wound Ado if he resisted leaving her, especially if the albularyo was skilled. Worse yet, Genie might not survive the fight should he resist and could possibly die.

'What's going to happen now?' he asked himself. He was afraid that if he posed that question to Ada, she would crush him too much with the truth. *There must be another way. I can't lose her.*

'I can't . . .' Ada started floating up. *'I can't do this anymore,'* she said to him.

Her pain made sudden sense to Miguel as the memory of the life he once had with Ada started creeping back into his mind. He could feel it, rolling like a fog over the illusion of his life with Genie. He remembered being happy with Ada but wondered, was there love? Real, consuming, all-encompassing love? The kind that he knew now. How could he return to his old existence without it?

'I'm leaving.' Ada hovered above the aisle and floated over Genie. *'Don't you dare take her back with you, Ado, or I'll tear her to pieces as soon as she sets foot in our realm . . .'* she said as she made her way to the window *'and the life that's inside her too,'* she added before disappearing into the dark.

He saw it as soon as the words trailed off her mind and into his. He saw it.

His child with Genie.

A beautiful and kind creature, just like her mother. She would move in this world with otherworldly grace and possess an inexplicable ease at growing anything from the ground. When she'd want to feel whole, she would find oneness with nature but when she would want to know love, she would embrace her mother and beg her to tell the story of when she fell in love with her father. Her real father.

Genie would then tell her a ghost story full of wonder and hurt. Of a time in her life, a long, long time ago, when she felt protected by an unknown force she could neither see nor hear. An entity that made her feel a love so powerful that when it went away, it left with a profound emptiness that only the love of her daughter could fill. It wouldn't make sense to anyone else, but for the mother and daughter, it would be the love story of their lives.

The vision made Miguel weak, and he started to weep. He bent over Genie and wished to be able to hold her in his arms, but his spectral limbs would just slip through her body, denying him of the comfort of a final embrace.

Oh, Genie . . . I'm so sorry. He hovered on top of her, his face a whisper away from hers. *I never meant for things to end this way.* He leaned over and kissed the cold air drifting on top of her exposed cheeks.

'I don't want to leave you but it's the only way for both of you to survive this. Never forget me, my love.'

Genie opened her eyes and heard an echo of a voice lingering faintly in her ears. She sat up and looked around the cold, dark bus for a few confused seconds before she was able to recall where she was and what she was doing. She was on an overnight bus from Manila. She was on her way home. But something was different. For the first time in a very long time, she realized she no longer felt like she was being twisted in a knot. Her limbs felt as if they'd been disentangled and whatever it was that was weighing her down was somehow gone (or left?) and she felt inexplicably, released. But how? And why now?

She thought back to her phone conversation with her mother. Perhaps she'd been right about the Maligno. Genie hadn't taken her seriously about seeing an Abularyo but now she knew she should. Something else was at work here. Something malevolent. Something that might come back, renew its chokehold on her life once more, and never let go.

She turned to the empty window seat next to her and immediately noticed a covered Styrofoam cup wedged in the mesh pocket of the seat in front of it. She took it out carefully, struck by the sudden need to quench the dryness in her throat. When she lifted the cover off, the odour of warm bone broth wafted into her nose. She was abruptly overcome with intense revulsion. She quickly covered her mouth, shoved the cup back in the mesh pocket and scrambled down to the front of the bus.

'Manong!' She managed to say to the bus driver before another intense turn in her stomach made her lurch forward. The driver took one look at her and immediately understood. By the time he maneuvered the bus to the side of the road and opened the bus door, Genie had vomit running down her arms. She spent another few minutes heaving on the side of the road. When she finished, she noticed that some of the passengers had disembarked to stretch their legs and were eyeing her with annoyed curiosity.

When she finally stopped retching, the bus driver who had been standing at a close distance walked over with a clean rag and a bottle of water. She offered a weak word of thanks and an apology for delaying everyone.

'Don't worry about it, Miss!' the bus driver said. 'My wife gets like that too when she's pregnant.'

'Oh no, I'm not,' she quickly corrected him, but then her chest tightened and a voice inside her mind whispered, *That's not true.* A wave of panic surged through her.

'Ay, sorry, Miss.' The driver smiled, embarrassed. 'Well, if you're okay, you can get back on the bus and we can get going?'

Genie was suddenly struck with dread. The thought of being pregnant made her blood run cold. It was impossible, she'd never been intimate with anyone and yet . . . it took her a few more minutes of just staring at the confused bus driver before she managed to nod at him and go back inside the bus. When she got back to her seat, the first thing she noticed was the uncovered cup of broth that had triggered her nausea in the seat pocket in front of her. The sight of steam still rising in tiny curls from the cup made her skin crawl. Just then, the substitute driver walked up the aisle to count heads and make sure that all the passengers were inside the bus. She immediately grabbed his arm and handed him the cup.

'Manong, please, can you throw this out for me please before we drive off?'

Her intensity startled him for a second before he took it away from her. Genie watched him walk off with it to the door and continued to observe him closely until she saw that he walked back in empty-handed. Only then did she begin to feel better. When the bus finally got going again and the lights were turned off, most of the passengers settled back down and began to doze off again.

Genie, however, decided that she was going to stay awake until she reached Camalig. She checked the time on her phone. Four hours to go before she'd be home. She'd sleep after she visited the albularyo and found out exactly what was happening with her. Until then, she dared not close her eyes. Whatever it was, she was determined not to let it slip back in and take over once more. Genie drew the curtains open, said a quiet prayer of protection, and then looked out into the dark night with guarded apprehension.

The Waiter

Dubai

The first thing Julius noticed when he opened his eyes was the sensation of burning. His skin felt tight, as if it had been stretched over a flame and singed. He ached deeply, not just on his skin but in his bones. Stranger still, his skull felt as if it was pushing against his scalp. He realized he was standing up. This was strange because his last memory was of him lying down, or more accurately, of him falling.

In the distance, he heard terrified shrieking. When his vision eventually cleared up, he realized that he was standing in the desert. It was nighttime and the screaming was coming from Nikhil, who was a few metres away from him, crouching on his knees, screaming at him. From what Julius could see, Nikhil was covered in blood and sand. His shirt was ripped, his pants and underwear were half down to his ankles. He was screaming with a terrifying intensity that made Julius' blood run cold.

I'm dreaming . . . this is a dream, he thought. What else could it be? Nothing made sense and his memory was foggy and full of questions. Where exactly was he? What was he doing here? What had happened?

He thought back hard, but all he could recall, his last memory, was from a few days ago, when Nikhil had suggested that they make their way to their secret hideout in the desert to watch the supermoon.

'We should go to our spot to watch it!' Nikhil had hardly been able to contain his excitement.

The idea of watching a full moon event filled Julius with dread. Immediately, he was assaulted with images of his parents forcing a small, black bird into his mouth when he was a child. 'This is who we are,' his mother had said like an incantation. 'It's the only way,' she had added. Meanwhile, his father's hand had been clasped tight over his mouth. 'This is so you will go through the change, anak.' As if the violation was a normal thing. Julius' skin crawled at memory of that black bird slowly twisting inside his mouth, choking his desperate cries for them to stop. The taste of membrane and feathers, as vivid on his tongue as the day it happened. 'The full moon asks for it. The full moon demands it,' he remembered them chanting in unison.

'Fuck the moon!' he had hissed at Nikhil.

Nikhil ignored his tantrum and playfully leaned in to grope him instead. 'Come on! It will be so romantic.' Julius immediately stiffened at his touch but pushed him away in terror.

His boyfriend had then walked away, cackling merrily, as if what he'd just done wouldn't get them into trouble.

'Are you crazy?!' Julius had hissed at him. It was noon during the middle of the week, and they were—on one of their rare days off together—at his favourite public beach in Jumeirah. There was no one but the two of them in the men's washroom. Still, he'd rather be overcautious than incarcerated.

'Nikhil, you crazy asshole, don't you ever do that shit again!' Julius had yelled after him.

He remembered Nikhil nagging him about it several more times as the moon event neared. He remembered saying no just as much. He had even lied about his hours at the restaurant, insisting that he was on shift to close up that day and would be too tired to go out.

So, how did they end up here? This place he had said he didn't want to be in—their hideout in the desert. The same spot they'd gone to numerous times before. The only place in Dubai where they could get some privacy, be intimate, and most of all, be themselves.

Julius thought hard and it slowly started coming back to him.

Somehow, despite his protests, they ended up in the desert. He recalled lying down on the large imitation Iranian carpet they had picked up at Carrefour and the moon looming so large above that it seemed as if it was about to descend on top of them. Its size and weight sucked all the sound from the sand and bathed them in glorious moonlight. It almost made him forget how deceitful the moon could be. For once, it seduced him. They kissed. Then, by force of habit, Julius looked around like a guilty criminal despite the remoteness of their location.

His paranoia made Nikhil laugh. 'We are in the middle of nowhere, Julius! Relax, babe.'

'Correction. We are in between Dubai and Sharjah, which, to my knowledge, is still in the Middle East. They kill gays in the Middle East, you know.'

'OH EM GEE, my drama queen!' Nikhil feigned affectionate exasperation. 'I don't care what you think.' He leaned back to stretch his lithe body on the carpet before announcing, 'This is the best place on earth! Better than any five-star hotel!'

Julius struggled to relax. A sensation that had become rare for him in the past few months at work, where he logged in sixteen-hour days. Add to this the aggravation of constantly waiting on drunk, abusive western expats for a measly 1,500 AED a month, half of which got sent to his parents in Bicol to assure them that he hadn't been burned at the stake . . . yet. He had begun to feel like a rat on a wheel that was going nowhere. A hopeless vermin furiously working to power the very machine that would eventually kill him.

Thankfully, Nikhil was earning a decent enough salary as a manager to support both of them. Otherwise, he would have either given up and gone back to Bicol or died of exhaustion— poor and even more broken than when he had first landed in this messed up country. Dubai was changing him. He could feel it. He noticed how every little thing had started to bother him. Every little thing became a big thing because if there was anything Dubai was good at, it was reminding everyone at every possible opportunity that unless you had money and were a westerner or an Emirati, you were nothing.

Being treated like nothing had exhausted him to the point of rage, and the rage had been creating a version of him he didn't like. Someone he didn't recognize, someone out of control. Conveniently, it would come to a boil every time he was behind the wheel or whenever a big fancy SUV cut into his lane. Nikhil had referred to these instances as his 'nuclear meltdowns'.

'Julius, you need to calm down! What's the point of throwing a tantrum over it?' Back in the desert, Nikhil's head had moved to occupy Julius' lap. 'That was hours ago. Are you still pissed off about that lady? *Khalaaas* . . . let it go.'

Earlier that evening, they had nearly collided with a Porsche SUV on their way to the desert. The female driver hadn't even stopped; she even had the nerve to wag her manicured finger at them as if it was their fault that she had carelessly barrelled into their lane without signalling. Her pricey car could have crushed their dinky Toyota Vios like a tin can.

'Wouldn't it be wonderful if we could do something about it though?' Julius bristled. 'I'm done with this fucking town's arrogance!' A mixed expression of disgust and frustration had settled on his face.

'Do what? Tell off every bad driver on the road until you're blue?' Nikhil laughed and added, 'You've been so sensitive, lately Mr Crankypants!'

'We could shoot them. Just shoot all of them,' Julius announced, as if he had just had a light bulb moment.

Nikhil turned to him with amusement. 'Yes! Like just get a gun and shoot everyone on the road! Brilliant idea.' He continued laughing.

'No, not just shoot everyone on the road! We just pick out the ones who commit traffic violations. You know, like the ones who cut into lanes without signalling, people texting while driving, the speeders, the lane hogs, the assholes who flash their lights at you, so you get out of their way. Just drive after them and shoot them!'

Nikhil clapped his hands with pretend glee. 'I love it,' he giggled. 'Best idea ever! When do we start?'

'First, we need a gun,' Julius responded as if he was considering it for real.

That was when it happened, Julius was certain now. The moment that brought them there, hurting and confused. The memory came to mind like a blow to his head, and he nearly lost ground.

A ricochet of hot wind zipped in front of them. He recalled how they both bolted up in panic. Then, they looked down at the object that had flown past them—a thin syringe with a colourful tail lying on the carpet. It looked like a plaything Julius had once kicked around for fun as a child in the Philippines. In the distance, they heard a chorus of voices. Julius recalled hearing laughter, which made the blood drain from his face. He began to panic. *This is it*, he thought. They'd been caught. They were going to jail. He was going to be burned at the stake.

'We should go,' he recalled saying to Nikhil. Fear crept out of his throat and into his voice.

'Hello? Who's there?!' Nikhil yelled.

'Shut up?!' Julius turned to Nikhil, stricken with fear. Just then, a sharp pain shot up his left thigh.

'What's wrong, Julius?!'

He looked down at his leg and saw another syringe with a similar bright red feather sticking out of his pants. The sight made his body go limp and his legs gave way from under him. He dropped on the carpet like a rock.

Nikhil kneeled beside him. 'What's happening? What's this? Julius?'

Julius reached down to his leg and pulled off the syringe. 'Get out of here Nikhil, QUICK!' he said without realizing that he had begun to slur his words.

In the distance, he remembered hearing more laughter, it sounded like a group of men (or was it boys?). Moments later, another syringe landed just inches past Nikhil, who had been so worried about Julius that he hadn't even noticed that he was a target too.

'RUN!' Julius grabbed Nikhil.

Then, everything faded to black.

It was Nikhil's hysterical screaming that brought Julius back.

'Nikhil,' he called out to him except that the voice coming out of his mouth didn't sound like his voice. What he'd said didn't even sound like a word. He stepped forward and fell over a body. When he looked back at it, he realized that it was a headless torso. He was holding the head.

He tried to scream but what came out of his mouth was a wet gurgle that made his skin prickle. In the distance, he could hear Nikhil's screams edge deeper into horror. He threw the head away in revulsion, when his eyes caught sight of his hands. Could they still be called hands? He looked at the pair of twisted leathery claws that were attached to him. Running his gaze down his body, he realized with horror that his foot had turned into a cloven hoof. His skin, obsidian black.

What was happening? His heart was pounding in his chest. Inside his head, he heard the voice of his mother chanting, 'This is who we are, Julius.'

'No.'

His tongue, now thin and slick, whipped the word like a snake inside his mouth. This was not happening! He screamed in his thoughts. The black bird, the full moon, all those years ago when he came of age. It didn't happen then, so why now? His mother had been so disappointed. He stood up on uneasy hind legs and towered over the blood-soaked sand.

In the moonlight, he could see severed body parts strewn around him. If only his mother could see him now. No wonder Nikhil was screaming. He turned to him again. The movement was enough to make Nikhil bolt up and attempt an almost laughable getaway. He stood up to run but his pants were bundled around his ankles, and he fell back down, exposing his bare ass in the moonlight. This was when his screams turned into desperate wailing.

Julius was instantly overcome with the need to rush to him and calm his terror.

'Nikhil, it's me!' Julius moved closer.

'NOPLEASEDEARGODPLEASENO,' Nikhil begged in one breathless shriek. Somehow, he managed to successfully push his pants off and then immediately took off half naked into the desert. Julius ran after him, calling out his name, the syllables stuck between grating monstrous vocalizations and his natural voice.

They ran aimlessly in the desert with Nikhil screaming into the emptiness.

'HELP PLEASE SOMEBODY HELP!'

Then, not even 100 metres into the chase, they both fell. Tumbling all over each other from the peak of a sand dune. When they rolled to a stop, they both noticed the faint glow of a campfire in the distance. Julius could neither see anyone around nor could he smell anyone else apart from Nikhil. It was the blood. Oh, dear god, he could smell it, down to the pulsing riot in Nikhil's terrorized veins. His parents hadn't told him anything about being able to smell or feel blood moving. It was a disturbing new discovery among many other disturbing things that evening. He dreaded finding out more.

But first, he needed to convince Nikhil that even though he was a grotesque monster barrelling towards him, he was not dangerous. He watched Nikhil rush inside the empty camp and followed after him yelling (or gurgling), 'Please stop!'

'STAY AWAY! PLEASE DON'T KILL ME!' Nikhil begged. He grabbed a piece of a log that was lying next to the bonfire and started swinging it at Julius.

'Nikhil, please. It's me, Julius!' Suddenly, he sounded like himself again. The sound of his real voice was so unexpected that it made Nikhil stop swinging.

Julius walked slowly to him. Relieved to finally stop and take in the desperate state of his poor lover who was looking at him with confused, horrified eyes.

'Julius?' Nikhil asked in exhausted disbelief.

'Yes, it's me.' He started crying. 'I'm so sorry.'

Suddenly, the sobs came pouring out of him. 'I didn't know . . . they told me I wasn't one. I'm so, so sorry.'

He moved in closer with outstretched arms, but Nikhil swung the log once more and backed away. The reaction broke Julius' heart and made him weep even more. He didn't even realize that his sobbing made him sound like a wounded animal.

'How is this possible? What are you?' Nikhil was still holding the log up, eyeing Julius with a mix of intense bewilderment and fear. 'What is happening, Julius?! This is a dream! Are we dreaming?' he said, shaking his head.

'I wish we were, Nikhil,' Julius said in between sobs.

'If it's really you, then prove it to me.'

Julius looked at Nikhil teary-eyed and thought for what seemed like an eternal moment.

'You have a tattoo on your left rib. It's in Hindi and it means love. I have the same thing too.' He pointed at his bare left rib with bloody claws. That was when Nikhil dropped the log. He walked over to touch the tattoo on Julius's leathery chest and then collapsed in a heap in front of him.

With that, Julius fell down too.

They remained crumpled in each other's embrace, weeping some more before Julius turned his attention to the active bonfire in the middle of the camp. An SUV was parked on the side but there was no one around, and it seemed abandoned. Julius was confused when he realized that the camp spot smelled oddly familiar to him. It wasn't a feeling of having been there before but more of a familiarity with the stink. Either way, he couldn't quite decide if it was safe for them or the missing campers.

'You haven't answered my question, Julius . . . What are you?'

What was he? It was a question he couldn't really answer without thinking of his parents. After all, he had asked the same of them when they had told him about the family secret all those years ago.

'What's an aswang, Mama?' Julius asked his mother. He must have been six or seven years old when he first became aware of this word. His recollection took him back to their home in Sorsogon with his mother, who, at that moment, was toasting a bowl of shredded coconut for the Tinutungan she was going to make—his favourite.

'Where did you hear that word?' she asked, with no hint of alarm or surprise. She just kept blowing air onto the small pieces of charred black charcoal inside a mound of shredded coconut she had piled on a ceramic bowl. It created a thick plume of sweet smoke that danced around her delicate face.

'Aling Basya at the *palengke*[19] said that I'm the child of an aswang.'

'Who said that?' His father came around from corner. 'Aling Basya at the palengke,' his mother answered him. Again, with that same indifferent coolness.

His father looked at him, studying his face intently. 'Well, he is of age,' he then announced, addressing his mother.

'I know that,' she said. 'But we still have to wait for the blood moon before we can do the conjuring.' Julius didn't exactly know what was going on but the exchange between his parents made him feel somewhat excited. It felt like he was

---

[19] Market

getting to celebrate his birthday earlier than usual and had gifts to open. 'I'm of age? Does this mean I can get ice cream?'

'No.' His mother immediately crushed his swelling excitement.

'Did you get the ginger like I asked you too?' she asked instead.

Julius' head dropped. 'I didn't,' he said shame faced.

His mother looked up from the smoky bowl of coconut and set it aside. She walked up to him. 'And why not?'

Julius started trembling. His mother had that effect on him.

'I heard Aling Basya say that . . .' Julius hesitated 'that she doesn't sell to . . . aswangs.'

'That filthy pig.' His mother snickered with amusement. She looked up at his father, but he remained quiet, only nodding his head to show that he agreed with her.

'I heard her say to Mang David that I'm cursed. God has cursed us. Why are we cursed, Mama?'

She turned back to Julius. This time, she had a confusing expression on her face that he couldn't quite read. Something between a smile and a sneer. *At least*, he thought, *she's not angry with me any more*. He stopped trembling and started listening.

'Julius, anak . . . we're not cursed. In fact, God has created us to be the guardians of this land. You know, a long, long time ago, people like Aling Basya were considered pests, like insects! Do you know what happens if you let pests breed?' Julius immediately thought of cockroaches when his mother said the word pest. The sight of one was enough to send him screaming into a corner. Sometimes, they even flew. The thought of them breeding made the little hairs on his arm stand on ends.

His mother continued. 'They bring disease and ruin to everything they touch . . .' she looked at him with a grave expression. 'If you let them breed more than they have to, they end up killing the land. You know how your dad and I tend to our crops so that that the land we live on can grow plenty of pili and abaca?'

Julius nodded his head. 'Well, if not for aswangs, greedy pigs like Aling Basya will end up destroying everything. They have no respect for nature. They care nothing about the land that houses and feeds them!' Julius could feel her anger building.

'Remember Julius, we are the guardians of this land. We do our part to make sure that the nature surrounding us continues to flourish. And we do this by making sure that it is free of pests, free of poison.'

'So aswangs are not bad, Mama?'

Her face softened. 'Not at all, Julius,' she said warmly. The change in her disposition made Julius smile.

'Then, I'm proud to be an aswang!' he announced.

His father started laughing. 'I wouldn't say that out loud if I were you.' Julius turned to his amused father with confusion. Why wouldn't he be proud if aswangs were good for the land?

'Also, you're not an aswang. Not yet, at least,' his father added.

'I'm not? When do I get to be an aswang, Mama?'

She stood up and went back to her bowl of shredded coconut. 'Soon, Julius. Don't you worry about that.'

'Mama, when I become an aswang, I will tell Aling Basya that she's wrong about us. I will show her the good that aswangs can do,' Julius added proudly.

'Julius, when you turn into one of us, I'll personally make sure that you show Aling Basya how good it is to be an aswang,' she said with a sly smile and resumed stoking the charcoal in the shredded coconut bowl.

'I'm what they call back home an "aswang". A werebeast. I'm a monster, Nikhil,' Julius said looking down at his claws. He turned them back to front and thought back to what his mother had said all those years ago. *These are not the hands of a guardian, Mama*, he thought to himself. He wished she was there right now to make sense of everything.

'What does that mean? You're a werewolf?' Nikhil asked, stupefied and uncertain about how to respond to Julius' answer. 'Are you going to bite me? Are you going to kill me too?'

'No, no Nikhil. I've already fed, I think . . . You're safe.'

Nikhil recoiled. '*Hai Bhagwaan!*[20] This is not happening!'

'Nikhil, it's still me in here. I will never hurt you!' Julius wanted to pull him back into his arms but thought twice about reaching for him again.

'How did this happen to you, Julius? How did you turn into this . . . thing?'

Julius didn't want to answer any more questions. What he wanted to do was to get away from the desert, wait out his mutation, get cleaned up, and hide. Nikhil seemed hurt and could need medical attention. He needed to take him to a hospital, they needed to get back to their accommodations.

'Julius, I need to know, please . . .'

Then it dawned on Julius. He couldn't do any of those things. There was nowhere to go when he was in his aswang form.

---

[20] 'Oh my god!'

'Julius are you listening to me?! Tell me, how is this happening!'

Nikhil then started blabbering incoherently. It took a moment for Julius to realize he was speaking in Hindi. Babbling while sucking in deep breaths, as if he was drowning in his own words.

'Nikhil, please . . . breathe. You have to calm down.' The proposition sounded ridiculous, and he realized that even before the words left his mouth.

'Calm down?! Look at yourself Julius. Look at me!' Nikhil pointed to himself. They both looked at Nikhil and realized that Nikhil was still half naked.

'Oh my god, look at me.'

Nikhil was suddenly silenced by the sudden awareness of his condition before finally asking,

'Where are my pants?' He was genuinely perplexed.

Julius was about to tell him how he lost his pants when Nikhil's face collapsed. He started to sob again.

'Those pigs. Those fuckers,' he cried.

Rage bubbled underneath his despair. He turned to Julius. 'Four of them came out from behind the dunes. I couldn't leave you.' He paused and struggled to clear the cry stuck in his throat. Julius trembled with the frustration of not being able to take Nikhil into his arms and comfort him. His real arms, not these gruesome monstrous limbs.

'Two of them dragged me away from you and just started punching, kicking me. It happened so fast. I couldn't . . . they were stronger than me.' He wept.

It was more than Julius could bear. He walked over to Nikhil and held him with his leathery arms. This time, Nikhil didn't even flinch at Julius' touch. He settled in Julius' embrace weeping.

'I didn't know what they were doing to you Julius. One moment, I thought I was going to die and the next moment there was this scream that stopped everything. I thought it was you.' Nikhil paused, recollecting. He looked up at Julius who, in his aswang form, towered a good foot above him.

'Oh my god. You saved me.' He had just come to this realization. 'What you did to them? They deserved it.'

There was an angry satisfaction in Nikhil's voice that made Julius feel better. Right now, he would rather settle for an angry Nikhil than a fearful Nikhil. He thought back to earlier in the evening when the first dart had struck him. He remembered falling, a second dart whizzing past, and then losing control of his body. Somewhere in his foggy brain, he remembered male voices approaching and Nikhil screaming, followed by heaviness on his chest. As if there was something or someone on top of him.

Then, it came back to him.

A man breathing in his ear, his breath smelling of stale cigarettes and sour liquorice. He could smell a whiff of it now, standing in the middle of that camp.

'This is where they made camp,' he said to Nikhil. It made sense now. The camp was empty but not entirely abandoned. More importantly, there was that familiar smell. Julius broke off from hugging Nikhil and started walking around the still smouldering campfire. The flame was just right enough to keep the charcoal in their shishas burning. He thought of them huddling around this fire, smoking while planning to brutalize them. Had they been watching them for long? Had they perhaps seen them go back to their spot in the past, when he and Nikhil had been intimate before? Had they planned this assault thinking, 'Who will care about two gay Asian men?' In hindsight, Julius realized they were easy prey. What these pricks didn't count on was unleashing a predator. None of it mattered now, they were in pieces all over the desert and he and Nikhil still had to figure out what to do next.

Nikhil watched Julius circle the bonfire. 'We should get out of here,' Nikhil said. His voice was heavy with unease.

Julius started making his way to the SUV parked next to camp, a white FJ Cruiser. He grabbed the front door, expecting it to be closed. It opened easily.

'Julius, what are you doing?' Nikhil went over to him.

'You need pants,' Julius said as he started searching inside the car.

'The people who camped here might be coming back Julius. Hai Bhagwaan! I didn't even think of that.'

Julius turned back to Nikhil. 'They're not coming back, Nikhil, they're dead.'

'How do you know that?! Are you sure?' Nikhil looked around the camp, searching for any sign of other people.

'Nikhil, trust me. They're dead.'

'All of them? What if there's more?'

Julius paused, raised his snout to the night sky and announced. 'There's no more, Nikhil, and if there are, I'll kill them too.'

Julius turned back to the SUV and started looking through the contents of the vehicle. This time, a kind of switch had flipped inside his mind, and he went from despairing to trying to survive this night. They needed to somehow get to their car parked on the side of E84 without attracting any attention but with the moon this full he may not transform until early morning.

They'd have to wait until morning before they could make a move. Maybe it was possible for them to get out of this situation quietly. No one knew that they frequented this spot, and no one could possibly think that what killed those men could be human. The thought was enough to make Julius feel somewhat hopeful. Then, just as immediately, he quietly scolded himself for even considering that life could still be normal for him and Nikhil.

Nikhil took his cue from Julius and walked over to help him. Together, they found several bags, blankets, bottles of water, and junk food. Nikhil started opening the bags looking for clothing. 'We can use the car to get out of here,' Julius said to Nikhil. He glanced over to the ignition hoping that their attackers had also left the keys but no such luck. They'd have to go back up to their spot and look for it among the mangled body parts.

'Julius. Oh my god, look at this!'

Nikhil pulled out a wad of passports from one of the duffel bags. The documents looked like they were from the US, Canada, and the EU. However, none of the passport pictures were of westerners. Some passports even had similar pictures.

Julius looked at it anxiously.

'What does this mean?' Nikhil muttered, grabbing the other bags and pulling out the contents. He looked through a wallet and found a leather case with identification in both English and Arabic. It had a picture of a very serious looking, bearded young man. Nikhil stared at it intently, trying to discern if it was one of their attackers.

'I think these guys might be criminals,' Nikhil said and continued digging into the bag.

'It doesn't matter Nikhil! Just find a pair of pants so we can get out of here,' Julius said with exasperation. Nikhil nodded in silent agreement.

They continued going through the car until they finally found some random bits of clothing in the trunk. Some shirts, a jacket, and then, finally, a pair of loose pants. Julius grabbed it and by doing so, uncovered a sight he'd never really seen except in movies. He was looking at a cache of guns. Seven? Maybe ten? Most of the pieces were big, long and deadly looking. He'd never seen guns like this before. He stared at them in disbelief before uttering a bewildered wow.

'What is it?' Nikhil walked over to him. '*Madarchod*,' he cursed. His eyes were wide with astonishment. Julius picked one of the bigger guns up. 'Its heavy!' he announced with childlike surprise.

'What are you doing?! Do you even know how to use one of those things?'

Julius grabbed the assault rifle by its pistol grip and magazine, rested the butt stock against his shoulder and squinted along the barrel. 'No,' he finally said to Nikhil. 'But this is how they hold it in the movies!' Meanwhile, Nikhil had grabbed the pants Julius had found and tried them on. Fortunately, they fit. *At least*, he thought, *something is right*.

Julius was still holding the assault rifle when Nikhil grabbed one of the guns himself. A shiny revolver with a black handle. It reminded Nikhil of something Shah Rukh Khan might use in one of his films. Nikhil held the grip with both hands, looked at Julius, and thought about how strange it was to find themselves in this situation. Assaulted in the desert, playing with guns. He was about to share this with Julius when he noticed something different about him. He seemed shorter and less hairy. Less like an animal but still not quite the normal Julius he knew and loved.

'Julius? I think you're changing back . . .'

'What?' Julius relaxed his hold on the assault rifle and looked down at his body. It was true, it really did look like he was changing back. His fingers seemed to have lost its claw-like hold, while the thick black hair on his skin appeared to have retreated. He was also hunching less and standing a bit more upright. Maybe it was because he was aiming a gun? He looked up at the moon, still bright and enormous against the black sky.

He didn't think he would be changing this soon and he didn't really feel any different. But then what did he know about being an aswang? Thinking back, he'd never really seen his parents go through their transformations. After several excruciating attempts at initiating him into the family 'heritage' had failed, his parents hadn't shared any further information about their kind with him. Growing up, he had made the decision to ignore the sound of his parents feeding on poor pregnant women from other barangays. Even on the evenings when they would tear into each other, fighting over who would get to eat the foetus this time, he never dared look. If he didn't see it, then it was not real. He regretted not knowing much and if he was going to be honest with himself, he regretted not knowing anything about what he was. Julius knew then that until he spoke with his parents, everything would remain a mystery, and anything would be possible.

Just then, a sharp stabbing pain clawed through his insides. He doubled over, lost his grip on the assault rifle and fell to his knees. Nikhil dropped the revolver and knelt next to him with renewed panic. '*Chutiya*![21] What's happening now?!'

The pain was excruciating. For Julius, it felt like his stomach had turned into a bladed creature that was attempting to cut its way out. The sensation made him howl in agony before he doubled over spasming jerkily. He could actually feel his blood simmering against his skin.

Nikhil started to weep again.

'Julius, what's happening?' Nikhil cried, helpless and terrified. 'Tell me what to do please.' Nikhil had barely finished saying the word 'please' when Julius' spasms turned into violent vomiting. His body regurgitated a thick black goo that made a wet, splattering sound as it landed in chunks on the sand. It made Nikhil recoil. It looked like oil, and it looked alive. *So, this was how it feels when evil passed through you,* Julius thought. It felt like giving birth to death. He felt like he was about to die and even if that didn't happen tonight, he wondered with dismay if it was going to be like this every time he went through the change. He stayed on his knees, alternating between shrieking in pain and heaving for what seemed like forever until he felt something like a smooth stone pass through his mouth. It landed in the congealed black sludge a few metres away from him. He stared at it breathless, drained, and inexplicably, unburdened.

'Julius . . .' Nikhil crawled back to him, a look of recognition and relief on his face.

'You're . . . you,' he said. Julius did not just look like himself, he finally felt like himself. Wearily, he inched closer to the stone he had just disgorged and almost gasped at what

---

[21] *Chutiya* is a curse word in Hindi.

he saw. A smooth black stone in the shape of a chick lay on the sand. He'd seen it before. On the many nights in his childhood when his mom would force it down his throat.

'Hey!' called a male voice—young and agitated—from a distance. 'What are you doing here?' he demanded.

Julius and Nikhil both turned in his direction. They saw two young men on their dune buggies parked just a few metres away from the camp. One dismounted, and in a hail of angry incomprehensible phrases, started walking to them. Julius attempted to stand up but immediately fell back down. 'I'm sorry, Nikhil.' Julius looked at his lover, defeated. Nikhil didn't say anything. He calmly bent down to pick up the revolver they had found and aimed it at the young man who was now stomping his way closer to them.

'Stop!' Nikhil screamed and then, the gun went off.

The young man clutched his right ear, screaming as a burst of blood sprayed down his neck and his fingers.

'Wafey!' his friend called out behind him. Nikhil looked back at Julius, dumbfounded.

'What are you doing!?' Julius yelled at him.

'I didn't mean to! The gun went off!

They heard the dune buggy start up. Nikhil aimed his gun in the direction of the other man, expecting him to drive straight to them. Instead, he manoeuvred his buggy the other way and quickly disappeared into the dark. Julius watched him speed off and thought, *We're done.*

There was no getting out of this quietly now.

Nikhil then aimed his gun back at Wafey, who was now screaming with increasing rage.

'Stop! Please,' Nikhil yelled at him. 'Stop screaming!'

To Nikhil's surprise, he did stop. Wafey looked at him with insane eyes, said something incomprehensible, and furiously moved towards him. Nikhil pulled the trigger repeatedly until the barrel emptied itself completely into Wafey. The sound of gunshots was still echoing around the dunes when Nikhil collapsed next to Julius. He threw the revolver away and stared at Wafey's bloody body lying just inches away from them in disbelief.

'Chutiya,' Nikhil cursed, defeated.

Julius wrapped his arm around Nikhil and pulled him close. He strangely wished he was in his aswang form again.

'What do we do now, Julius?' Nikhil asked, not realizing that he'd started crying again.

Julius wiped the tears from Nikhil's face and said, 'Well . . . let's get back on the road.'

He struggled to stand up on shaky legs but managed to walk over to where the black stone gleamed like a jewel on the sand. Once he'd retrieved the stone, he walked over to pick the revolver up from where it was laying on the sand.

'We're taking this gun,' Julius said, turning back to Nikhil. 'Now, let's go. At this time, traffic is going to be hell,' he said and held out his hand to his distraught boyfriend.

The Seafarer

Qatar and Albania

[An excerpt from the Albanian newspaper *Gazeta Express*]

26 August 2022
Wreckage of *Dasolca Gem*, a luxury yacht owned by suspected Russian crime boss, Maximov Dementev, was found in the Ionian Sea 110 miles from the port town of Durrës. The wreckage was discovered by Albanian fishermen who rescued a lone survivor clinging to the ship's debris. The survivor is a Filipina who worked as one of the crew. The survivor was taken to Durrës Regional Hospital, where the local police took her statement.

Police note that Ms Eugenia Mayor sustained no major injury but advised further examination and treatment for possible trauma and shock based on her emotional condition. Upon further

interrogation, the survivor revealed that
she had been hired as part of the housekeeping
crew on the sunken yacht, reported to have
been missing for four days.

When the police asked for her full name the second time, she
had to think about it. Ever since Ruding had started calling
her Enya, she had never thought of calling herself by any
other name. She certainly liked the sound of it better than
Eugenia Ludovice Mayor. Enya—the name made her feel
special, made her feel like she belonged. The police, however,
had insisted on finding out the rest of her name. She didn't
understand why Enya was not enough for them when it had
been enough for everyone else on the boat. Remembering
made her so sad. She'd thought that perhaps getting back to
the ocean would have made her feel better. Would have made
her forget.

[The following has been gathered from Durrës police
transcript dated 25 August 2022]

Taken from the interview and observation
of the *Dasolca Gem* survivor and witness.
Survivor to be kept under Durrës police
custody pending advice from Interpol in
connection with the criminal activities of
Maximov Dementev, her employer. Ms Mayor
was advised of her rights prior to making
her statements.
    Survivor is Eugenia Ludovice Mayor.
Twenty-four-year-old native of Daraga
Albay, Philippines.

Ms Mayor was contracted to work for six months by Premiere Yacht recruitment agency on the boat *Dasolca Gem* as a housekeeper/laundry stewardess. No supporting paperwork was found on Ms Mayor to confirm her identity.

According to her statement, she began working on *Dascola Gem* in June 2022. Ms Mayor does not recall exactly how many people were on the boat at the time of the incident but to the best of her knowledge thinks that there were about ten crew and ten guests, including the owner, who she refers to as boss Max (Maximov Dementev), onboard when the yacht went down.

Ms Mayor was asked to recall Mr Dementev's activities leading up to the accident and recalls the following events:

Ms Mayor claims that the boat was docked at a port in Doha (Ras Laffan) and had been there for a week before leaving for their next destination. Everything was proceeding as normal. The crew met for a briefing with the chief stewardess, identified by Ms Mayor as Ms Janet Blasius, a Swiss national. The crew briefing occurred immediately after breakfast wherein Ms Blasius went through everyone's responsibilities before the arrival of Max Dementev and his associates.

Enya had noticed that usually when leaving the Middle East, cargo would be loaded onto the boat and said cargo would be offloaded at their next destination. This happened consistently while she worked on the boat. She knew what was inside, so did everyone else. But no one really talked about it. At least, not openly. That morning, however, she had missed having breakfast with Ruding who, along with the other deck hands, was called to help load the cargo. Normally, the deck hands would leave this task to Ruding while they'd nurse their hangovers over greasy eggs and coffee. Enya figured there must be a lot of cargo her time if it required everyone to help.

> When asked whether she saw Mr Dementev and his associates bringing in drugs or weapons on the boat, Ms Mayor claimed that she witnessed weapons and cash of different currencies being carried into the boat in big boxes. Sometimes, there would be blocks of powders and medicines (pills) in crates. She notes that most of this cargo would be kept locked in the guest rooms but that sometimes there would be too many boxes that some (specifically the cash) would be placed in Max Dementev's master bedroom. Ms Mayor was asked to recall any other unusual incidents on the boat during her time working for Mr Dementev.

Truth be told, everything on the boat had been unusual for Enya. However, the repetitive nature of her duties soon made the unusual, usual—even if none of it made sense. Linens, for example, she never understood why linens had to be used for meals or why there had to be so many napkins. Nevertheless, it was her job to make sure that all the linens that were going to be used during meal service with Boss Max and his guests—from the tablecloths to the napkins—were clean, pressed, and pristine.

It was a never-ending process that began from the moment Boss Max exited the boat. In fact, the days leading to Boss Max returning to the boat would be the busiest for Enya. While everyone else would be preparing to go on shore leave to decompress and see the sights, she would be busy washing and drying all the laundry used on the boat. From bed to dining linens, bathroom and kitchen towels to the crew's uniforms. After making sure that every item was clean and stain-free, she proceeded with pressing every piece—a task that would take hours. This would be followed by folding, which, thankfully, was one of the few things that she didn't have to do standing up. She'd never been good on her feet and often wondered if she'd ever develop what everyone on the boat referred to as 'sea legs'—a phrase she found particularly amusing.

Folding laundry would also allow her to slow down from her never-ending tasks and—when she was really lucky—enjoy the company of her only friend on the boat, Ruding. When he was not busy himself, Ruding would come down to the laundry room to talk and help her with the folding.

He was not very good at it. Even after she'd shown him many times how to create the right folds and creases with specific shirts or towels, Enya would have to redo everything herself. But she didn't mind. Talking to Ruding, a fellow Bicolano, felt like being back home. She imagined it must feel like finding land after long days stuck at sea.

This was also when they would talk about all the things they would do with the money they'd earned working on the boat. Ruding would do most of the talking. She didn't mind that either. It excited her to listen to all the amazing things he planned to do with his hard-earned money. How he would buy his own boat and rent it out to day trippers along the Embarcadero in Legazpi city. She liked watching him become more animated when he would talk about just how special his tour boat would be. Insisting that it wouldn't be like any other cheap boat trip. It would be first class, inspired by the *Dasolca Gem*. His crew mates would wear uniforms, they would greet guests with a special Lambanog cocktail, and they would have fancy finger food versions of Bicolano delicacies. Ruding had it all figured out and listening to him talk about it made her feel like she was part of his dream. That was, until she asked him what he would name his boat. Enya was disappointed to hear him say the name Kristina. She couldn't hide her disgust and Ruding teased her about being jealous. Heat rushed to her face so fast that she left the laundry room without saying a word. Ruding chased after her to apologize for being insensitive. Then, he compared her tantrum to that of his little sister, which, Enya admitted, made her heart hurt even more.

During these times Ruding would also mention how happy he was to finally have a friend on board. Especially because he didn't really like anybody in the crew, not even the other Filipinos who worked in engineering. Ruding confided in Enya about how he probably wouldn't even have hung out with those guys at all if he wasn't stuck working on the boat with them. Meanwhile, he was treated like dirt by the bosun and the other deckhands. Most of the time,

Ruding would complain to her about working with a bunch of lazy, alcoholic guys who made him do most of the heavy deck work while monopolizing the favourable shifts. He told her that sometimes it got bad enough, exhausting enough, and depressing enough that the money didn't feel like it was worth the constant abuse. Sometimes, he just wanted to throw himself in the ocean and swim home. But then he'd come to his senses and submit himself to the punishing routine once more. He only really needed to think about what awaited him back home to realize that the money *was* worth the abuse. If he gave up, he was not just giving up on himself and his dreams of *Kristina* the luxury boat tour in Legazpi, but the dreams of his family. From his mother, his father, his brothers, to his cousins. Enya felt the weight of his responsibilities, his resilience in the face of anguish and without realizing it, fell deeper in love.

Ms Mayor claims that Mr Dementev and his associates arrived at around 10 a.m. that day but that she wasn't on deck to witness the arrival. By then, she had finished her tasks, and the linens were taken to the dining area to be laid out in preparation for lunch service. Mr Dementev was expected to arrive with his female guests. She notes that Mr Dementev would normally have around two or three female guests with him. The girls would never be the same, but they were always tall, very beautiful, and very slim. They would be from different countries, *from either Africa, Asia or*

Europe. One girl, however, was always
the same. She was identified by Ms Mayor
as Kristina Samuel, a Brazilian national.

Kristina was perhaps the most beautiful woman Enya had ever seen. She had long, dark, honey hair, big breasts, a tiny waist, and a curvy ass (ass was a word she struggled to identify until the men talking about it made hand gestures that indicated the shape of her behind). Kristina's ass would inevitably become the topic of much lascivious conversation among the men on the boat. She noticed how they almost seemed to salivate in between bites of their meals while describing her 'ass' or pounded harder on the table when they talked about having enough money to pay for just one night with her. This, at first, confused her, since she had always assumed that Kristina was Boss Max's wife, and all the other girls were his girlfriends until Ruding explained Kristina's role on the boat to her. He emphasized that everyone had a role on the boat and that for Kristina, it was to keep Boss Max happy. Then, with a wink, he added that his role was to keep Kristina happy with his special 'powers'.

He left before Enya could get him to elaborate on what he meant exactly by his 'special powers'. Not that she wanted to know more really. She may not have worked on boats as long as the others, but she'd heard stories of how Filipino sailors would keep women happy and it was not through anything she thought should be called a special power. Although, she did want to know exactly how *bolitas* on a man's penis could make a woman happy. What special power could tiny plastic balls have that would lead to happiness? She decided that she would insist that Ruding give her a better explanation next time.

Ms Mayor states that on the day of the incident, Max Dementev arrived with only Kristina as his female companion, which she claims was unusual. She adds that his usual security detail was with him. Eight men who normally carried small guns when they arrived but then switched to bigger and longer guns when they were out in the open sea. When asked if she knew the identities of the eight men, Ms Mayor says that they were neither introduced to the crew by Mr Dementev nor did the men introduce themselves to anyone. When pressed for descriptions, Ms Mayor noted that some might have been Arabs, but the rest seemed to be of European origin.

NOTE: Interpol to send pictures of known associates for identification by Ms Mayor.

It amused Enya that they thought they needed the guns to protect the boat from pirates when there were scarier things out in the sea. She knew this for a fact. She knew guns would not protect them at all.

Ms Mayor claims that it was just before lunchtime when Rodolfo Misolas, a Filipino national and one of the deckhands, came down to see her with distressing news. He said that the boat had sailed off without the chief stewardess Ms Janet and Sir Denis Claves, a Macanese national, identified by

Ms Mayor as the head chef. According to Ms Mayor, Rodolfo Misolas had asked the captain about their whereabouts but was told not to worry. He had been told that both crew members would join them in Albania, their next destination. Ms Mayor identifies the captain as one Nuryev Galkin, a Russian national. Ms Mayor notes that this had never happened before. She adds that they had always sailed as a complete crew. However, Ms Mayor says that this was her first job on a private yacht and she's not sure what was usual and unusual, but she still believed the deck hand when he said that something was not quite right.

She had never seen him look so fearful. In place of his usual, easy-going cheekiness was a creeping paranoia. Like a relentless force of water, Ruding's fear reminded her of stormy waves. An inevitable tide that kept pushing him down into the deep dark sea, no matter how hard he tried to keep his head above it. Enya didn't quite know how to soothe his fears. He kept asking her questions that made no sense. It seemed as if he was really asking himself these things, not her. 'Do you think he knows? But how can he know? Unless she's told him! But why would she do that? She would get into trouble herself!' Enya figured Ruding knew the answer to his questions and that was what was really scaring him.

Ms Mayor claims that after lunch, Mr Dementev retired to his bedroom to take

a nap, which was part of his routine. He
would normally get up just before 3 p.m. and
ask for his usual vodka martini and caviar as
an afternoon snack. Meanwhile, Ms Kristina
would be on the sun loungers in the upper
deck.

Enya was convinced that the upper deck was where Kristina
must have bewitched Ruding. She could see it vividly in her
mind. Kristina lying down on the loungers wearing next to
nothing. The throne on which she spread her sensuous shape
to weave her trap of lust and desire. No hot-blooded man in
his horny mind would not want to be caught and entangled.

It was easier to think of Ruding's seduction this way. He
couldn't help himself; he was helpless against his desire. Just
as she was helpless against her feelings for him. So helpless
that she was lured into leaving her world and crossing the
barrier into the other.

Ruding didn't know it, but he had seduced Enya himself. He
had called out to her with the force of his longing. He did this
whenever he yearned to be back home instead of retiring in
his cramped windowless quarters in the lower deck. Whenever
he craved boiled pili with patis alamang instead of the crew
meal. Whenever he wished he was singing karaoke with his
brothers during a family get-together. The more Ruding felt
the anguish of homesickness, the louder his loneliness called
to her. She couldn't resist it. It was a siren song that opened the
door between his world and hers.

Unlike most seafarers on ships, Ruding didn't pine away
for the love of another woman back on land. Enya didn't care
much for the weak and banal desires of seafarers for their

girlfriends on land. The taste of their longing always made her feel insignificant and unwanted, not like the omnipotent sea creature that she was—a terrifying, moon-swallowing behemoth who had inspired stories and myths. Even the name they had given her sounded terrifying. Bakunawa. In all honesty, most of it wasn't really true. Well, at least not the moon part. The moon was her navigational guide! She couldn't really eat the one thing that helped her find her way.

What she did eat, what sustained her existence in either world, was the exquisite loneliness of people at sea. Whether it was big or small ships, the loneliness of seafarers on these watercrafts was a delicacy unlike anything she'd ever tasted. Mostly because of what it was really made of—love.

For every man and woman longing for home and family, was a human being sending out waves upon waves of their love for their wives or husbands, sons and daughters, fathers and mothers, pets and yes, even food. All that yearning, craving, aching fervent desire flowing out of their lovelorn hearts and into the sea where the Bakunawa could swallow it all and feel loved herself, even if it is love for other people.

As for this form of Eugenia Ludovice Mayor, a young newlywed who worked as a chambermaid for one of the big cruise ships crossing the Mediterranean. Like Ruding, she too sent her loneliness out to sea. She sent it to her equally young husband back home who, she had later found out (four months into her deployment) had started seeing another woman and was going to have a child with her. The Bakunawa knew of this because she had found Enya's body floating not far from the waters that the *Dasolca Gem* often passed through. Her bloated corpse had still been in the cruise liner's uniform when the Bakunawa decided to swallow her whole, absorbing not just her flesh but also the crushing heartbreak and despair that made Eugenia throw herself off the ship.

> According to Ms Mayor the day proceeded as normal up until she was called to assist with the dinner service. She also notes that Mr Rodolfo Misolas was called to wait on Mr Dementev and Ms Samuel while they dined. She claims that this was unusual, as Mr Dementev preferred to be served by the white crew. Ms Mayor claims that Mr Dementev seemed particularly interested in Mr Misolas that night, asking him many questions about himself while he served the food. Ms Mayor states that although Mr Misolas successfully completed his task of serving food, he was trembling the entire time.

The Bakunawa never intended for things to get as far as they had. At first, she was quite content feeding from Ruding's loneliness from a distance. But the longer she fed on his yearning, the more she wanted.

She thought of the day she had come upon Eugenia's body floating in the water. It had felt like fate. She had seen an opening in the cosmos, an irresistible invitation to make her way to the other side. It was no coincidence that two individuals from the same region in the same country had somehow presented themselves to her at the same time and place. It seemed serendipitous and too remarkable to not explore. The Bakunawa wanted to know what it felt like to have something in common with another being. To share familiarities and affiliations. To experience their loneliness deeply, intimately. What she hadn't counted on was experiencing the emotional bondage that humans referred to as falling in love.

> Ms Mayor claims that just before serving dessert, Mr Dementev asked Mr Misolas if he had been stealing from him. This caused Mr Misolas to drop the plates he was carrying and fall to his knees to the floor. At this point, two of Mr Dementev's security men grabbed him by the arm and placed him on a chair facing Mr Dementev. Ms Mayor claims that Mr Dementev asked the crew to leave the dining room. She notes that Ms Samuel tried to exit with the crew but was asked to stay behind. Although Ms Mayor had left the room with the crew, she claims to have continued observing the incidents in the dining room from the kitchen porthole.

The Bakunawa had not realized how she felt about Ruding until he confided in her about Kristina. Normally, she enjoyed sitting and talking with him for hours, but that day, his revelations struck her like a flash storm. Every word felt like a lightning strike to her heart. Every detail became a sobering wave of cold, hard truth that washed over her, reminding the Bakunawa of what could never be.

Ruding's affair with Kristina started during one of the rare shore leaves he had managed to take. They were docked in Montenegro, and he was at a local café drinking his homesickness away after another emotional video call with his family when she walked in. Ruding said that he almost hadn't recognized her. She didn't have any make-up on and was dressed very differently from how she was normally dressed when she would board the boat with Boss Max. Ruding thought she still looked stunning. In fact, he thought she looked even prettier. At first, he couldn't believe that she had even noticed him on the boat at all, much less recognized him. She asked if she could join him for a drink and before he knew it, they'd been talking the whole day. They ended up meeting every day at that very same café for more than a week.

As luck would have it, their schedule was postponed, as Boss Max was delayed with business and could not board the boat for a few more days. This gave Ruding and Kristina more opportunities to meet up and get to know each other. During these meetups he learned that they actually had a lot in common. Like Ruding, she came from a small town, she was the sole breadwinner in her family, and she also dreamed of starting her own business. 'A skin care company,' she said, 'one that only uses natural ingredients.' She even revealed that Boss Max had promised to finance her business after she presented him with a business plan. Ruding was impressed. She was smart too! He beamed proudly.

The Bakunawa listened and mourned silently. She hated herself for being so stupid, for allowing herself to hope and think that anything could ever come out of her feelings for Ruding. She had even been on the verge of confessing to him. It made her hate herself even more. Most of all, it made her hate who she really was—a monster.

Through the kitchen porthole, Ms Mayor claims that she witnessed Mr Dementev strike Mr Misolas across the face repeatedly with an empty wine bottle while two of his security men kept him restrained on the seat. During the assault, she claims to have heard Mr Dementev ask how long Mr Misolas had been stealing from him. Mr Misolas denied the accusations. At some point, Ms Mayor witnessed one of Mr Dementev's security men leave the room and come back with parcels of what looked like drugs and money. According to Ms Mayor, this was when Mr Dementev became even more agitated and instructed one of his security men to point a gun at Mr Misolas' head. Ms Mayor claims that the sight of her friend in mortal danger distressed her so much that she lost consciousness. Her next recollection was waking up while floating among the *Dasolca Gem* debris. She did not know how long she'd been in the water when the fishermen spotted her. When asked whether knows what happened to the other personnel on the boat, Ms Mayor became emotional and was unable to continue the interview.

NOTE: Interview concluded 30 August 2022 at 8.43 p.m. Durrës Regional Hospital. Further questioning advised in connection with Maximov Dementev's activities and movements prior to the incident. The Philippine Consulate in Tirana has been

It was only after the police left her room that the Bakunawa allowed herself to cry. She replayed the scene in her head over and over again, wondering, each time, if she could have done things differently.

She had lied to the Albanian police when she said she had been peering from behind the kitchen porthole.

The Bakunawa had, in fact, locked herself in the lower deck laundry room while the rest of the crew cowered in their respective cabins. They were left with no other choice. Boss Max's security men didn't even have to say anything, they simply waved their big guns to usher the crew out of the dining room and close the door. No one said a word, no one did anything, they just silently walked back to their quarters like there was nothing unusual at all about leaving a crew mate restrained in a room full of armed men.

The Bakunawa herself hadn't known what was going to happen exactly. She only knew what that room felt like in that moment—full of fear, suspicion, and rage at a boil. She called out to Ruding before being ushered out, but he would not look at her. He only shook his head and kept his head down.

Down in the laundry room, the Bakunawa allowed herself to use her basilisk senses to see what was happening in the dining room. She had to be careful and restrained. Otherwise, she would begin to change and return to her natural form. This is what would always happen when she used any of her dragon capabilities in human form. Regardless of what was happening, she knew she was not ready to transform back yet. She was not ready for Ruding to see her as she really was.

The Bakunawa silently watched as Maximov turned his attention to Ruding once more.

'Well, Ruding I've gotta hand it to you,' she heard him say. 'You've got balls if you think you can get away with it.'

When Ruding lifted his bloodied face, the Bakunawa gasped at the woeful sight of him and lost control of her ophidian hold for a brief moment. It made the boat hull shudder. She quickly tried to calm herself. 'Not yet, not yet, not yet,' she repeated under her breath.

Blood began to run down Ruding's mouth from where he had been struck with the bottle.

'Boss Max,' Ruding pleaded. 'I would never steal from you. I have never taken from you. I swear!'

Then, the Bakunawa saw him steal a look at Kristina as if to say, 'Please help me.' The Bakunawa watched as a look of panic suddenly appeared on Kristina's heavily made-up face. It was the ugliest she'd ever seen her. She sensed her sweating through her usual tight dress. She could smell it rising off her, a whiff of expensive perfume laced with the scent of fear and treachery. Hate began to bubble up inside the Bakunawa.

'Why don't you search his room to see if he has been stealing, sweetie?' She heard Kristina say.

Ruding began to nod in agreement. 'That's right, you will see that I have stolen nothing. I have nothing to hide!' he exclaimed, convinced that he would be proven innocent soon enough.

The Bakunawa watched Boss Max signal to one of his security men, who left immediately after Ruding told him where to find his cabin. Then, he stood up, grabbed another vodka bottle by the dining room bar, and poured himself a drink.

'The thing is Ruding', Maximov said while sitting on one of the bar stools, 'you have been stealing from me.' He lit a cigar he'd pulled from his jacket pocket. 'You see Kristina? She's beautiful, yes?' he asked, in between puffs.

Ruding and Kristina shared a knowing look. 'Yes?' Maximov repeated loudly, waiting for an answer. 'Yes.' Ruding meekly answered back.

'This beauty belongs to me Ruding,' he said. Then, through gritted teeth, Maximov added, 'So why do you think it's okay to fuck her, huh?' Ruding hung his head and stayed silent.

The Bakunawa watched as Kristina began to rise from her chair but one of the men moved to push her back down. She began to plead with her lover.

'Maximov . . . please . . .' she cried as her face turned pale despite her heavily rouged cheek.

Ruding began to cry. 'I'm sorry, Boss,' the Bakunawa heard him say. 'I'm sorry,' he repeated, choking on his words this time.

She watched as tears began to run down Ruding's face before the Bakunawa realized that she too had started crying. It made her want to save him right then and there. To take him away from all this fear and suffering and carry him with her on her giant back. She would take him back to Legazpi, where he could be with his family and would never have to leave home ever again. He would no longer miss out on any important, happy occasion. He could work on his dream of owning the best tour boat in Legazpi. And he wouldn't call his boat *Kristina,* he would instead name it after her, he would call it *Enya.*

Enya finally made the decision to reveal herself when she saw the security man who was sent off to Ruding's quarters return to the room. In his hands were envelopes full of cash and a box of what looked like white powder.

'I found these in his room,' the security man said and threw them on the table in front of everyone. Ruding looked at the items in terror. 'Those are not mine!' he screamed, rising from his chair. 'I swear!'

Maximov started laughing. 'I know, Ruding. I know.' He fixed his eyes on Kristina, whose mascara had started running down her face from crying. 'Right, Kristina?'

She shook her head from side to side. 'No! No, Maximov! It's him, it's Ruding. I've seen him stealing from you! He said he needed it to get his own boat!'

Maximov rose from his stool, flew across the room, and grabbed her by the neck. 'I'll make you see why you should have never stolen from me!' he snarled. Then, he lifted his hand and stubbed his cigar in her left eye.

Enya could hear Kristina shrieking all the way down in the laundry room. 'Don't lie to me you stupid cunt! I've seen the security footage. What do you take me for? An idiot?' Enya watched Maximov scream at Kristina. He then dragged her by the hair and pushed her down on the floor next to Ruding.

'Please don't hurt her,' Ruding whimpered.

Maximov looked at both of them in disbelief and roared with laughter. Then, he turned to his men and said something in Russian. Enya, meanwhile, couldn't move. *How could Ruding still care for her? Did he still love her?*

'You know what?' The mobster turned to Kristina and Ruding. 'I'm not entirely unreasonable. I'm going to give you a choice.' He addressed Ruding. 'The money or Kristina?' he asked.

The question sucked the air out of Enya's chest. She sat up and leaned in with rapt attention. Like Maximov, she needed to know, desperately. Kristina continued to writhe in pain on the floor, too wounded to realize what was happening.

Enya watched Ruding lift his head up.

'I'm serious!' the Russian boomed. 'But you can only have one. I will allow you to leave the boat with only one thing. All this money,' he gestured at the thick wad of cash on the table, 'or Kristina?'

Ruding continued to look at his boss, searching for some truth behind the madness in his eyes.

'Well?' Maximov asked impatiently.

Ruding had just turned to look at Kristina when the gun went off. Enya had not noticed, but one of the security men had pointed a gun at Ruding while he was contemplating the options he had been given. The gun decided for him. Kristina screamed as Ruding slumped down off his chair and landed on top of her. Suddenly the air in the room turned dense and still. Enya watched half of Ruding's head fly off and land on the floor in bloodied chunks. Her heart stopped and then, it started expanding.

There was no avoiding it now.

Kristina became even more hysterical and tried to crawl away, but the same man who shot Ruding aimed his gun at her and fired once. In an instant, everything became eerily muted in the room. Maximov cursed in Russian and spat on Kristina's body.

'Clean this up,' he told his men who had already started grabbing the bodies off the floor. 'I'm going to the Jacuzzi. Get one of the crew to make me a drink. Maybe that cute Filipina laundry girl,' he added.

Before Maximov could leave the room, the boat began to shake and splinter. In that moment, Enya allowed the shattered parts of her heart to rage inside her body and grow. She gave in to the wrath. Most of all, she gave in to the sorrow of losing love. Her head crashed through the hull and her wings expanded, splitting the boat in two. A storm of debris and frigid salt water erupted all around them. Mamixov and his men clung to whatever they could find as they watched a dragon emerge above them in terrified disbelief. They aimed their guns to the sky only to be met with darkness and fury.

[Excerpt from *The Manila Times*, 2 September 2022]

Filipina survivor of yacht wreck missing. Albanian police confirmed at a press conference yesterday morning that the Filipino *Dasolca Gem* survivor, Eugenia Ludovice Mayor has been missing since August 31st. She was last seen at the Durrës Regional Hospital where she was recuperating after being found by local fishermen. Hospital employees claim she was last seen in her room. Ms Mayor had been cooperating with the police in connection with the boat incident and the criminal activities of the boat owner, suspected Russian crime lord, Maximov Dementev.

Given the influence and power of Maximov
Dementev, police are not ruling out the possible
involvement of Mr Dementev's associates in
Ms Mayor's sudden disappearance. Meanwhile,
Philippine consulate representatives have
vowed to keep the pressure on local authorities
to continue the search and investigation on
Ms Mayor's case.

It was around 2 a.m. when the Bakunawa finally found her way to an abandoned beach resort. She stood quietly on the edge of the shore, letting the water caress her bare toes. It made her feel better even when the sadness persisted. *It's time to leave*, she thought. She looked at the full moon hanging above the calm horizon in front of her and knew immediately what she must do. The Bakunawa slipped into the water and left Enya behind. She swam deep, surging further away from land until she found him. Ruding's corpse, floating like a ghost at the bottom of the sea. 'Its' time to go,' she said to him.

The Bakunawa opened her mouth and swallowed his body whole. All his memories came rushing back to life inside her body, filling her with peace and banishing her sadness.

'There it is,' she said, 'there's my love.' She remembered clearly now.

'Let me take you home.' She said as she began her journey, following the light of the moon.

The Part-timer

Hong Kong

Merle's toes had already started to cramp. She'd only been wearing her borrowed red stiletto shoes a few wobbly clickity-clacks from the elevator to her 'client's' room. Ten steps, maybe twelve. *Punyeta, it hurt.*

At least, she wouldn't have to wear them for too long. She attempted to wiggle her near paralytic toes to life and decided that the first thing she'd have to do was convince this guy that she was sexier shoe-less. He would believe this, of course, even though he had explicitly instructed Manay Girlie that he wanted Merle to come wearing red stilettos.

This had been two days ago.

'What's your shoe size?' Manay Girlie asked, surprising Merle with her gleeful enthusiasm over playing dress-up. What was not surprising, however, was Manay's excitement over Merle's decision to finally do a little part-time work. Especially after

Manay had been nagging her for months about how much money she could make with her beauty and natural 'allure'.

'If I have what you have, ay! I will have every guy in Lan Kwai Fong eating off the palm of my hands! I will make a killing!' Manay would say. She would also never fail to nag her about it every time they would catch up over their little piece of cardboard real estate on Chater every Sunday morning.

A killing.

Hearing the phrase made Merle smile. But she had promised herself a year ago when she eventually found work as a domestic in Hong Kong that she would stop killing. After all, what had being an Oryol given for her? Nothing but regret and the power to attract losers. The older Merle got, the more exhausting she found it. When Victor was born, she discovered that she'd rather use all her energy to take care of her son. She found it more satisfying than any kill. She sustained herself solely on his love and it was ten times more gratifying than feeding on the life force of men. Once upon a time, when people had still believed in her myth, she was a demi-god—but with a small 'g'. Smaller even, if you took into account that her mother was the bigger 'G' and her grandmother, the main 'G'.

Merle was under no illusion whatsoever that she was a celestial. At best, she was a water nymph, and her lineage was the only godlike thing about her. Despite this, she could admit that Manay Girlie was right. Merle did make a killing with her beauty and 'natural' allure. And the reliable weakness of men always made it so easy for her.

'It's just this once!' Merle insisted emphatically.

'Of course, Of course,' Manay Girlie waved her hand dismissively.

'I'm serious, Manay.'

'Yes, yes, just this once,' Manay repeated, semiserious, before digging back into her closet.

Merle couldn't completely blame Manay for her zealousness. The client had offered 15,000HKD for one night. An amount they both agreed was too good to pass up. Two nights ago, when Manay had rung her begging Merle to take the job on her behalf, she'd thought it was a joke. Who pays that much money for one night of sex?

'A rich, horny accountant!' Manay had giggled, a little too hysterically that it verged on crazy.

As luck would have it, he wanted to see her on a full moon. The one night when she was at her most irresistible. Merle took it as a sign. They agreed to split the pay evenly between the two of them, which meant they would each get 7,500HKD in cash. It was more money than Merle would have ever had. Ever.

Before having her son, Merle never had much need for money. She existed simply to feed on the flesh and souls of men she would seduce in the shadows. Back then, she was satisfied with only indulging her selfish whims and her narcissistic need to look eternally beautiful and young. It was a weakness her kind seemed to pass on with every generation. There was, however, only one cardinal rule. Never ever play with your food. Merle was doing just fine until Gener came along and inevitably changed everything.

Merle wished there was something she could say that would accurately describe just how extraordinary Gener was. After all, this was the man who made a celestial being fall in love, who made her deny the hunger and disturb the natural order of things. Yes, he was different; until he wasn't. Predictably, he turned out to be just like any other man—a liar and a cheat. A callous heart breaker. In the end, he was a better meal than he was a lover. The only good thing that came out of the time she allowed Gener to defile her body, was the birth of her son Vic. The real love of her life.

'Shouldn't I be getting more, Manay? After all, it is my body.'

'Here it is!' Manay turned around with a pair of bright red, high-heeled shoes. Merle eyed it curiously and wondered how she'd even manage to walk wearing what looked like red stilts with leather straps.

'Manay . . .'

'Isn't it beautiful? I bought it with the money James gave me when we . . .' she paused to recollect. 'Ah no, this was *after* our first date,' she winked at Merle.

'Here, try it on and see if it fits,' she said and dumped the pair on Merle's lap.

'Manay, did you hear me?'

'You're not changing your mind, are you?' Manay Girlie took both of her hands and held them close to her chest, her face so close Merle could see the lines knotting her forehead.

'How much more will you need? He is my client, after all. You wouldn't even have this chance if he hadn't offered it to me first. 8,000? 9,000?'

Merle could do so much with that money. Just thinking about buying the PlayStation she could finally afford and sending it to Vic made her heart swell with motherly joy. Two days ago, it had been inconceivable for her to even consider doing anything like this. But the money was too big and her guilt over being an absentee mother too great. Greater than the shame of pretending to sell her body.

'My body . . .' the words trailed out of her mouth. She suddenly felt cheap and unworthy of her kind.

Manay Girlie thought she sensed apprehension in Merle's tone. 'Hay, you're so lucky. I'm on my period! Otherwise, it would have been my body,' she said squeezing Merle's hand before letting go. 'Okay, okay, you get more. Nine thousand for you and that's as far I can go.' Then, Manay went back to digging inside her closet without even waiting for Merle to agree with her.

Ah yes, the period excuse, Merle thought. Manay wasn't on her period. She would have smelled the blood on her. But why would she lie to her?

'So . . . James doesn't like having sex with a woman on her period?' she asked, playing along.

'Haye, naku Merle! He finds the idea of menstruation absolutely disgusting. He won't even see me or want to be near me. It's a quirk, but some men are like that, no?'

Merle shrugged. 'Tell me more about James then.'

Manay sighed and then paused a few moments more before talking again.

'James? He's good looking.' She smiled when she said this. 'Very sweet . . . a bit chubby but not fat! Not fat at all . . .'

Merle attempted to construct a mental picture in her head as Manay continued babbling. Good looking, chubby but not fat, clean shaven, blue eyes, blonde hair, soft spoken, lonely . . . very lonely.

'Ay! I have pictures, pala!' Manay exclaimed upon remembering. She grabbed her phone and started scrolling through her photo library. Suddenly, Merle was confused about finding herself feeling weirdly excited about seeing a picture of her first 'client'.

'Here!' Manay shoved the phone in her face.

The picture had been taken in a bar. Probably in Wan Chai, the Hong Kong red light district where Manay liked to spend her weekends. James' face was red, flushed most likely from a night of drinking. He was grinning from ear to ear and had his arm around Manay. Though she didn't particularly think he was good looking, she sensed a hint of playfulness in his eyes. He looked easy-going and kind. At least, she hoped he was easy-going and kind. It suddenly dawned on her that she'd never used her influence on a foreigner before. What if her supernatural charm didn't work on this guy? What then? Actually have sex? A shiver ran up her spine.

'Pogi, no?' Manay asked playfully. Merle nodded politely. 'Manay, for 9,000 he's Piolo Pascual.'

'Ayyyyy, you're so right!' Manay cackled hysterically. Her reaction so infectious, Merle couldn't help but giggle along with her.

'Now, I've already told you about using the condom. It's very important! Insist, okay? You tell him, no condom, no boom boom. He knows but, you know,' she paused and rolled her eyes, 'men!'

Merle pretended to understand. 'Yes, no condom, no boom boom,' she repeated.

Her skin crawled at the possibility of having to actually engage in 'boom boom'. She didn't even know how to work a condom. Her stomach turned.

'Also, he will ask you to drink. You know these gweilos, how they like their drink. Do you drink vodka? Oh, there's also cocaine.' Manay looked worried.

'Cokane, Manay?'

'Well . . . think of it as crushed medicine but you snort it up your nose instead of swallowing it. Instead of curing sickness, it cures . . .' she paused to look for the right word, 'shyness!' Manay explained, pleased with her own cleverness.

'So, it's drugs.' Merle had thought as much.

Manay could sense the creeping distress in Merle's voice. 'Yes, yes but try it, really! It will help you so much. It's really not that bad. Especially since you know . . . this is your first one, okay?' Condoms, alcohol, drugs. Merle felt her initial resolve fading fast. She heaved a heavy sigh, closed her eyes, and thought back to the last time she'd seen her son.

She had worked a full year before she had gotten to hold him again. A full year of twelve-hour days, no vacations, and sleeping in a room the size of a closet. A full year of profound loneliness, of caring for strangers when she should have been caring for her own. Could she have made it easy for herself by using her powers of persuasion? If her Amo hadn't been a single working mother struggling to take care of two kids and an ageing mother herself, perhaps she could have. But Merle understood her struggle all too well. Besides, her power only really worked on men, and only when the moon was full.

The one thing that had kept her going throughout the year was the thrill of eventually splurging all her hard-earned money on Vic. She was going to make all the punishing work she had endured worth it and had their special day all planned out. First, Merle planned to surprise him at school and bring him gifts. She had delighted in imagining how he would tear through his presents like he would if he had received them on his birthday or Christmas. Then, she would take him out for a Happy Meal, just like she used to when she would come into some extra cash in the past. Except, this time, she wouldn't have to say no if he wanted another sundae or even more fries—his favourite.

Merle thought back to that day when she had finally come home and landed at the Daraga airport. She hadn't even stopped to drop her luggage home, opting, instead, to immediately arrange a ride to take her straight to Vic's school. It was recess when she came up to the school gates and she immediately spotted him.

The sight of him was enough to instantly erase the anguish of her first year in Hong Kong. He was standing close to a group of boys who were passing a box of french fries between them. The sight of him almost made her gasp. He was taller and skinnier. Too skinny! He'd grown so much and the thought that she had missed out on all that time watching him grow, made her heart hurt with regret.

It was what she'd seen next that she summoned now to overcome her hesitation. Her boy reaching for a share of his friends' food like a street beggar and the woeful look of dejection his face when his friends refused to share with him. She focused on it, the memory of those kids laughing at his desperation. Merle zoomed in on his humiliation like you would on a camera. Until slowly, it turned her resolution into stone. Her shame at what she was about to do was turned into dust. She had started crying by the time she came up to him that day. After much hugging and kissing, she had bought him two Happy Meals and an extra-large fries to take home. It had crushed her to leave him again.

'Manay, you have to teach me how to put on a condom,' she pronounced with determination and started working the straps on the red shoes. Manay smiled widely, reached into her bag and produced a red box of Durex before announcing, 'This is so much fun! We should really do this more often.'

Fun was the furthest thing from Merle's thoughts when she finally made it to James' door. She cursed herself for deciding to wear the shoes in the elevator when she could have just slipped them on at his doorstep. Either way, she only needed to keep up this façade until she was able to say hello anyway. As soon as that happened, he was going to fall under her spell, just like every other man had when the moon was full and her beauty demanding of a sacrifice. This time, however, she planned to have a quiet night in some stranger's hotel room, passing the time watching a K-drama on Netflix while he drooled in the corner convinced he was having the best sex of his life for 15,000HKD. There would be no boom boom, no feeding, no sucking out of life force. Although if she was going to be honest with herself, the idea was very tempting. In fact, if this worked out . . .

Merle began to entertain the idea of compelling him to see her again. Just her, no sharing with Manay Girlie. She was smiling at her own shrewdness when the door suddenly opened in front of her. She hadn't even knocked yet. It was a moment so unexpected that it made he lose her balance and she teetered on her heels once more. Merle saw James' face only for a brief moment before she fell inside the room. Her 'hello' turned into a panicked 'ayputangina' as she hit the floor. Then, the unthinkable happened. She passed out completely.

She woke up choking. Before she could open her eyes, she felt a burning sensation in her mouth. Something was scorching her tongue with a low, searing heat that was making her gag violently. She was still on the floor with her chest down. She tried to move but realized that her hands and feet had been bound with ropes. Then, she discovered that the heat was coming from an unknown instrument that had been shoved inside her mouth and secured tightly with tape. A hard, tube-like device with a handle that was pressing down on her chin and an extension that was reaching the back of her throat. It tasted like plastic and oil.

'I thought that would wake you up.' His voice was calm, almost cheerful. Merle wanted to scream but every effort she made moved the object deeper into her throat. It made her gag even more.

'It's called a rabbit.' He chuckled and walked in front of her. 'That's what's making you gag right now, a rabbit,' he added, laughing this time.

Tears had started streaming down her face when he moved to sit cross-legged on the floor. His bare, dirty feet almost touching her face. Merle's stomach churned at the smell of human blood. She craned her head and tried lifting half her body up to look at him but was frustrated to find out that he was sitting too close. *Why did his feet smell of human blood?* she thought, her panic deepening.

'Look . . .' He shifted his hips away and held a box in front of her face for her to see.

'I picked it up yesterday.'

It was square box with a picture of a pink rubber toy on the front. The label read: 'G spot clitoris stimulator rabbit shaped vibrator. Now with heat feature!'

'I hope you like rabbits.'

To Merle, it looked like a toy figure with an oversized penis. He wasn't lying. A pink plastic bunny was fucking her mouth. Enraged, she started writhing on the floor in a useless struggle to get up. She sounded like a squealing, drowning animal. Her tongue unconsciously darted forcefully inside her mouth, attempting to eject the vibrator. It made her gag reflex kick in again.

He slapped her across the face. 'You better stop that,' he said, agitated.

She heard a clicking noise and then she felt the heat subside. 'See?'

He was holding a small round instrument in his hand. Merle could see that it was the same colour as the vibrator on the box. It also had the same tiny bunny-like ears.

'It's a wireless remote,' he said. 'I can be 10 metres away and still turn it on or off.'

He remained casually seated on the floor as he turned it on again and the object started vibrating. This time, however, Merle didn't make a noise. As her teeth and her jaw started rattling inside her skull she thought of Manay Girlie and her fury started to build. Did that bitch know about him and sent her off anyway? No wonder he had offered so much money. Then, a more heartbreaking thought. Manay had no intention of sharing the money with her at all.

He turned the remote off. 'You're different. I like you,' he decided.

Take off this fucking thing in my mouth and I'll show you just how different I am, she thought.

'You're also a little too early.' He stood up, placed the remote on a table behind him and walked up to her. Her heart started pounding.

'My delivery is coming in a few minutes,' she heard him say as he walked behind her.

'And right now, you're in the way.'

He grabbed both her feet and started dragging her across the wooden floor like a sack. She lifted her head, looked around, and spied the vibrator remote on the living room table along with cans of Red Bull and empty bottles of alcohol. The room reeked of garbage and vomit. Most of all, it reeked of death.

He dragged her a short distance from the living room into the bedroom, before dumping her in the bathroom tub. There was another body in the bathroom. Another woman. She was naked and crumpled next to the toilet with her head face down in the bowl. Merle couldn't tell if she was alive or dead. But with so much blood in the room, she was certain that a person had already been killed in there. Her breath quickened at the sight and the smell. She thought of the unimaginable. *Am I going to die here tonight?* For the first time in her life, Merle knew fear.

'I'm sorry about Janice,' he said, looking down at the girl before turning his attention back to Merle. James' figure was bloated and imposing in the bathroom light. Whoever he was when he met Manay was not the same person standing in front of her now. He was not the red-faced man with an easy-going grin at a bar in Wan Chai. What stood in front of her now was something else. Someone no longer human but a debased creature with wicked eyes.

In him, Merle saw a deeper well of perverse depravity and right now, he was only ankle deep in it. She could sense that he was eager to dive in full tilt. She knew this because it takes one to know one. For monsters like them, the thrill of bloodlust was too seductive to not indulge. There was going to be a feeding tonight after all, but whose appetite would be satisfied? If she only could get him to remove the fucking toy from her mouth.

He grabbed Janice's hair and lifted her head off the toilet. The poor girl's face was swollen and blue. A crusty trail of vomit and blood hung off her lips down to her chin. Merle saw her eyes flutter for a second before her eyeballs retreated to the back of her lids. She was alive, but barely.

'Janice, my favourite of all the girls,' he announced with satisfaction.

'I made her eat shit on this toilet, you know? She's my good girl,' he said, pleased with himself. He twisted Janice's head so it was facing him. Merle thought she heard her gurgle a word weakly. It sounded like 'please'. James looked down at Janice and, for a second, seemed confused. 'Oh wait, you're not Janice. Who are you?' He then turned to Merle again.

'You though, I can tell you're going to be a grade A pain in the ass.' He tossed Janice's head back into toilet like an unwanted toy and knelt to get closer to Merle in the tub.

'But,' he said, fixing his deranged gaze intently on her. 'I like you. Girlie was right, you are very pretty.'

With that, she met his eyes and understood. Manay had known and still sent her to be devoured by this beast. Had she known Janice too? Had she been one of her bar friends? Had they laughed for hours while they talked about men?

Tried on each other's dresses and exchanged stories about what they would do with their share of the money? Suddenly, Merle felt a familiar turning in her flesh. A growing rage in her gut that was summoning the demon in her. All she needed now was a touch of fresh water to begin her transformation. She imagined coiling her serpentine form around Manay and ripping her heart out. She would make Manay watch as she tore into her still beating heart. But first, this hijo de puta.

James pushed his hand into his jeans pocket and pulled out a small, plastic bag of white powder. 'I wasn't going to do this before my delivery, but something tells me you're a special one,' he said, smiling. He opened the packet and tapped a white line of powder on his forefinger. The whole line disappeared up his nose in an instant.

'We're going to have a lot of fun tonight.'

He grabbed Merle's hair, pulled it back, and tapped the rest straight into her nostrils. She accidentally inhaled a small amount before blowing most of it off her nose and back into his hands in a spray of white.

'You shouldn't have done that,' she heard him say before he slammed his fist into her left cheek. Her head hit the bathroom wall, and she reeled. The taste of blood flooded her mouth, and she panicked for a moment at the thought of passing out again.

Suddenly, the doorbell rang. 'Finally!' James straightened, excited. 'Don't make a sound or I will make you regret it!' he threatened as he looked at her like a delinquent child before turning around to walk out of the bathroom door.

The doorbell rang a few more times before she heard him open the door. Even with the ringing in her head and the throbbing pain in her cheek, she could make out another voice in the living room. Another male, impatient, restless but friendly towards James. 'Your place is a dump, man!' she heard him announce with obvious disgust.

James laughed it off before saying impatiently, 'Do you have my stuff or what?'

Alone with Janice in the bathroom, Merle started to weep. *Look at us*, she thought. *How did we get to this? Who did you have to endure this torture for? Your parents? Husband? Your child? And for what?* Merle studied the savage cuts on Janice's naked body and imagined the brutality and pain she must have suffered. Her face beaten black, her nipples sliced off. All this so that her daughter could get pretty new shoes? A big new HD TV for the husband, perhaps? Maybe a bigger house for her parents? *Which of them were you thinking of when you decided to take a chance, Janice?*

Merle's tears ran down her sweaty face and began to soak the tape over her mouth. She thought about her son and her weeping quickly turned to sobbing. *I'm so sorry, Vic. I only wanted you to have a better life.* She closed her eyes and remembered his face the day she had to go back to Hong Kong. The day his lonely, pleading cries broke her heart enough to make her momentarily lose her determination and consider staying home for good.

'I just want you to have everything, Vic. If I don't go, you won't get books for school or new clothes or new shoes!' She remembered saying. He had been unconvinced. He had held on to her harder, crying into her chest.

'If I don't go, you won't get that PlayStation that you said you wanted,' she had finally said playfully, but he'd only shook his head harder.

Thinking about that day with him suddenly strengthened her resolve. *If I ever get out of this, I'll come home again, Vic, and I'll never ever leave you again. I promise*, Merle thought to herself. She looked at Janice's body slumped over the corner and decided that this was not how she was going to die. This was not how she was going to go. No, not like this. Not if she could help it.

Merle moved her tongue around the object in her mouth hoping to shove it off once more. She felt a little give that hadn't been there earlier. Had her crying loosened the tape? Had the punch on her cheek moved the toy and created space in her jaw? Her heart started hammering against her chest, and she began to calculate how much time she had before James came back in.

She started to repeatedly push her tongue against the object with as much force as she could. Maybe she could move enough of it from her mouth to be able to vocalize somewhat. Enough, at least, to compel him to remove this abomination off her mouth and untie her. After that . . .

The door opened and James walked in. Just then, Merle felt a portion of the tape on her mouth rip a little more. Her heart stopped.

'Hello again, Janice,' he said as he came in. Merle thought he seemed less unhinged and more in control, but his eyes still glittered with violent anticipation.

He moved in closer, walking past Janice who was unconscious on the floor. This time, he had a long knife with him. Merle fixed her eyes on him and continued to frantically push the object from her mouth while she shrank deeper into the tub. She could feel the tape tear some more, but the object was still too deep inside her mouth to let her vocalize anything beyond panicked grunting.

James knelt down and held the knife to her face.

'You can stop that now. I know what you're trying to do, love,' he said, almost as if in a daze. Merle held her breath.

'Now that I've had my hit, I want you to suck my dick.'

He slipped the blunt end of the knife against her cheek and sliced the tape off her mouth. Merle looked at him in complete disbelief before she spit the vibrator out. It landed with a loud clang in front of her. A harmless looking thing really. Nothing but a toy coated in her spit and blood. James stood up and started to unzip his pants.

'Now, I want you to suck me good. If I feel you do anything else, I will jab this knife deep into your ear while you're down there. Are you listening to me?'

Merle cleared her throat, spat some more blood and saliva into the tub before she turned to him.

'No, James, you listen to me.'

James immediately fell into a trance. Her voice would be the most beautiful sound he would ever hear.

The Beauty Therapist

Dubai

It dawned on Loida as she bent down between Gemma's legs that she had seen more of her client's bush than her own. Right now, though, this wasn't the reason behind her agitation.

'I need a brazilian today,' Gemma said to her with a giggle in her voice and then added, 'My Papi is coming by later, so you know what that means.'

Loida did know what that meant and it filled her with rage. She felt it rise up her throat and flood her mouth with a bile of concentrated hate. She wanted to vomit on Gemma, to open her mouth as wide as she could so she could eject all the hurt that she was feeling right now. Straight into Gemma's unwaxed pussy.

Instead, she smiled. 'Yes, brazilian. Full? Or half?'

'He prefers the half look.' Gemma smiled wider.

Loida swallowed hard, responding with an 'of course' while pushing her anger down until she felt it land like a rock deep in her gut.

'Let me just see if the wax is nice and ready for you, okay?' she said and turned towards her workstation. Loida closed her eyes, took a slow, deep breath and checked on the consistency of the wax by stirring it around with a wooden popsicle stick.

Concentrate on the work. Concentrate. On. The. Work. The words echoed in her head as she willed her anger to melt like the red wax with each stir. Its colour and thickness reminding her of the consistency of blood. The deep crimson helped steer her focus on her to-do list. The real work that needed to be done. It was enough to make her smile, and her hand steadied soon after that.

'I'm so glad you could come today.' Gemma was lying down on her bed, next to the workstation Loida had set-up. She had the wax heating in a miniature slow cooker, neatly placed beside other beauty equipment that she had taken from the main branch of The Pretty Women Beauty Lounge—a one stop beauty centre where—according to the sign on the salon (spelled 'Saloon') door—everyone was committed to servicing the needs of Dubai's beauty conscious women. Right now, Loida was committed to providing a special discounted beauty home service in the privacy of Gemma's room. She had made the offer to Gemma in secret after she had finished Gemma's mani-pedi just a few days ago, confident that the girl would not resist a bargain deal.

Loida had learned a lot about Gemma in the months since she'd come to the salon for her regular beauty treatments. Even if, at first, she wasn't Gemma's preferred beautician. Then, one day, Loida was asked to wax Gemma's legs after her usual beauty therapist had called in sick—a case of food poisoning that Loida had arranged. She had done her job with servile professionalism, of course but it had sickened her to the core. In the end, however, it was worth the indignity. After that first session, Loida had turned into Gemma's preferred beauty therapist. It was an impressive accomplishment in more ways than one, considering, no less than three months ago, Loida had known nothing about nail spas, removing bunions, or blow-drying hair.

In training, Loida had impressed her employers so much with her efficiency and enthusiasm that she was now servicing clients faster than most new hires. She discovered that the desire for revenge was a powerful motivator that way. She used it like fuel, a kind of liquid loathing running through her veins. Without it, she wouldn't have kept her sanity through the unforgiving hours crouched over calloused feet, bent over hands and face-to-face with one too many hairy, smelly, and sometimes, menstruating, labias.

'I was so excited when he called to say that he was coming straight from the airport to see me. You know, it's been weeks and I've really missed him,' Gemma babbled. She was relaxed and talkative as usual, even with her legs spread wide open and her clit exposed. Her casualness had always unnerved Loida. Mostly because, despite herself, she found it quite charming. 'Papi' probably thought so too. She supposed it was one of the things that made him fall deeply in love with her. Deeply enough for him to lose touch with himself, along with his daughters back in Albay and her—his wife of three years.

His withdrawal from their lives happened slowly, his absence, in a blink. It opened a void that reduced their existence to a dot. A period that ended his time with them as a loving father and husband. Before he was Gemma's 'Papi', he had been Loida's Ruben. Two years ago, when they had sent him off at the airport, he was full of devotion and promises. She thought back to the moment when all four of them had huddled together in tears at the gate, overwhelmed with longing before even embarking on their separate journeys. Ruben had smothered all three of them with kisses and made emphatic assurances that he would ring or video call every day.

And so he had, for the first few months at least. Thinking about that moment now disgusted Loida. The deceit, the lies. It corrupted every good memory she had with him in the past and made her wonder if she'd ever truly known the man she'd been married to all this time.

After a year, the money he would send regularly turned irregular. He would miss a month or two and whine that his employers had not paid everyone at work due to reasons she could not really understand. Thinking back to it now, she realized that he had never gone into much detail about these things with her. But Loida never complained. She just accepted that things would be tight for a month and made do. She always made do.

Before marrying Ruben, she'd always been self-sufficient. Even with no college education, she had managed to support herself and her family with the money she had made as an accomplished albularyo, a folk healer. In Ligao, people would travel for miles broken with heartache and unexplained illnesses just to see her. They would seek her out for the potency of her natural cures, healing oils, and the most popular of all, her love potions.

But, for a lucky few, she was a gifted alchemist. When she was younger and single, she used to take pride in practising the darker aspects of her innate gift, even if doing so meant reaching for a power so malignant that she would feel defiled for days. A perverse kind of wickedness would take root in her soul, and she would need to remove herself from her family until the evil she had summoned passed through. Because of this, Loida would choose to create the darker spells only for extraordinary circumstances and certain people.

'Thank you so much for coming in on your day off, Jennie. Promise,' Gemma winked, 'I'll give you a big tip.'

Loida turned to her and attempted a sincere smile. Adopting one of her daughter's names when she moved to Dubai had been part of the plan. She was not quite used to it yet, but it reminded her of the sacrifices she'd had to make to be where she was right now. Yes, she had to temporarily leave her children behind, but she took comfort in the fact, that soon enough, it would all be worth it.

'Oh, don't worry about it. I should be the one thanking you. I need the extra cash because my eldest starts school next month and she needs new shoes.'

'Oh, you have a daughter?'

'Daughters. My pride and joy.' Loida beamed. The only genuine emotion she allowed herself at that moment.

'You must miss them so much.'

Loida nodded quietly, turned away, and busied herself with preparing the waxing strips. She refused to engage on the topic of her daughters any further. In her mind, this bitch wasn't worthy enough to know anything more about her life. Gemma, however, was oblivious and would have likely carried on babbling with or without Loida in the room.

'Who is taking care of them? Is your husband here or back home?'

'They're with my parents in Ligao. My husband,' she paused, unsure of what to say next, 'he's dead.'

Gemma gasped and sat up slightly. Loida couldn't tell if she had made the sound out of embarrassment or genuine pity.

'I'm sorry. How long ago did he die? Oh my god, I'm being too nosy . . .'

'Oh no, you're not really. He died a year ago. He was killed by a rare, flesh-eating bug that can only be found in Albay.'

'That sounds scary.'

'It is. the bugs are called Dermestidae or skin beetles. Have you heard of them?'

Gemma shook her head, curious to know more.

'"Derma" is Greek for "skin" because that's what they like to feed on. Human flesh. They don't look like much really, especially if you find just one. They're brown and this small,' she gestured with her forefinger and thumb, 'so they blend really well into rural areas, like where we live. They have these three tiny black dots arranged like a triangle on each wing. They're quite beautiful actually . . .'

'Oh wow, okaaay . . .'

'A female will crawl inside any opening in your body and then lay hundreds of eggs. When they hatch, the larvae are ravenous, and they start eating through the skin from the inside in a matter of days.'

'Ugh,' Gemma covered her mouth, 'stop. You're going to make me vomit.'

'At first, you'll start feeling this slithering sensation all over your body, as if worms are crawling just under your skin. You'll hear them creeping around in your skull, swarming in clumps to the softest part of your body. You'll feel them in your lungs, your eyes, your brain. The sensation will make you want to tear away at your skin. It's the pain though—'

'Jennie, please. I don't need to hear anymore.' Gemma started to gag.

'—the pain is unimaginable. When their tiny, greedy teeth start mincing your insides, they actually grow six to eight times bigger. They consume everything until there's nothing left of you but clean, white bones.'

Loida observed the queasy look on Gemma's face and watched warily as the horrified girl lurched and bolted to the toilet. She cursed herself silently for going too far too soon. It had taken her too long to get this private moment with Gemma. She wouldn't be able to forgive herself if she lost this chance now. She knew she might not get another opportunity to get this close to Gemma again. More significantly, she knew she couldn't stand to prolong the agony of keeping up the farce any longer.

'Oh no, Gemma. I'm so sorry!' She chased after her. 'I'm sorry. It's just that . . . I don't get to talk about what really happened to my husband that often . . . Gemma?'

Loida could hear her retching and coughing inside the bathroom. 'Gemma? Are you okay?' She heard the toilet flush. 'I feel so bad, let me throw in a free facial for you today after the waxing, okay?'

Seconds later, Gemma opened the door. 'Really? That would be amazing!'

Loida looked at her with relief and smiled. 'It's the least I can do after I just made you throw up with my story.'

'Oh my god, I can't believe that really happened to your husband,' Gemma said as she made her way back to the bed. 'Poor guy . . .' she said, lying back down.

Loida walked back to her station and looked into the small, boiling pot of red wax. She turned down the dial to reduce the heat and fixed a towel underneath Gemma's bare ass.

'Yes, poor guy . . .' she said as she reached for Gemma's legs and pushed them apart.

'Why don't you tell me more about your Papi? He sounds like a really nice man.'

Gemma settled back comfortably in bed and turned animated again as she started talking about her Papi. Meanwhile, Loida put on a pair of latex gloves and positioned herself between Gemma's open legs, eager to get started. She continued listening to Gemma as she whined about how hard it was to find a decent man in Dubai. About how she'd seduced Papi, even though she'd known he was married. Her voice even turned remorseful as she recalled how they tried 'really hard' not to fall in love with each other but that they just couldn't ignore the call of 'true love'.

Loida was screaming on the inside and bit her lip hard to distract herself. 'That's so sweet,' she managed to say through gritted teeth. It took all the willpower she had not to empty the whole container of hot wax on Gemma right then and there. Instead, she dipped the wooden stick into the wax, blew on it lightly and applied a thick smear around the lips of her labia.

'Is that okay? Not too hot?' she asked Gemma.

'It's okay,' Gemma responded placidly without even looking at her.

It won't be long now, Loida thought to herself. It made her think back to what had brought her to this moment. An encounter that had been made possible thanks to the wonder of social media.

It started when she hadn't heard from him in over two weeks. Something that had been happening with more frequency by that point, a year ago. That fateful day, she opened her Facebook account with the intention of leaving him yet another worried message when she saw that he'd been tagged in a photo by a girl called @itsGemmaDXB. It was an image of Ruben with a group of other men, red faced and grinning from ear-to-ear inside a restaurant in Dubai. She eyed the multiple bottles of beer on their table and the big silly hats they were wearing and thought that they must have been celebrating something. The sight of him happy and relaxed made her smile.

It would have been just another unremarkable photo of a few people having fun.

But the longer Loida looked at the picture, the more she realized that something about it made her stomach queasy. She read the caption.

'The gwapito boys! I'm in love <3 Papi.'

She looked at Ruben in the picture and realized that there was something different about him. He seemed younger, flashier even. His hair was cut shorter than usual, and his pricey looking purple buttoned-up shirt was something she didn't think he'd normally choose to wear in the past. There was something about the boldness of the colour that kicked off her anxiety. Like a stain that she couldn't rub off. It made the voice inside her head grow louder, telling her to move the cursor and click on Gemma's profile. She held her breath as she clicked to know more.

Loida ended up spending that whole day poring over every picture and detail on Gemma's page. Through it she discovered that Gemma used to work as a receptionist for The Pretty Women Beauty Lounge until she quit to become a receptionist at an engineering firm. The same engineering firm that had hired Ruben. She liked to go dancing with friends on weekends, she was obsessed with BTS, and she was in love with the new man in her life. In fact, she thought he could be the one. She called him her Papi.

In her pictures, Ruben may as well have been another person, he may as well have been this Papi. She studied every inch of their photos together and found that she struggled to recognize her husband. Not because he looked different from the Ruben that she knew but because she found it difficult to reconcile the image of him being so intimate and so uninhibited with another woman with the image of the man she'd married.

This could not be the same man who had promised to take care of her, provide for her, care for her and their children. This wasn't the Ruben who'd sworn that he would love and cherish no one else but her. No, not him with his arms around this slut sitting on his lap, her arms around his neck, laughing and smiling at him with adoration and vice versa.

She stared at that photo until her chest started closing in and then she wept from the excruciating pain of her heart breaking into shards. When she finally stopped shaking, she managed to leave him a message on Facebook.

Who is Gemma?

He called her soon after that. He started with an apology about not calling sooner because he was 'very, very busy at work'. To Loida, his explanation sounded like noise. A blah, blah, blah cacophony of excuses. She was only interested in hearing about one thing.

'Oh, she's just a receptionist at work, Loida!' Ruben said with a dismissive chuckle.

'I don't care if she's the CEO. They let people sit on your lap at work like that?'

'It was a company outing and we were all drinking! Everyone gets a little carried away, you know. She said I remind her of her brother, so it's harmless really!'

'She's in love with you, Ruben. She said so on her Facebook.'

'What? No, no, no. She's really young, so she gets easily confused.'

Loida wasn't convinced. 'You better unconfuse her then.'

'Loida, this is silly. You have nothing to worry about! You are my wife, I love you . . . Where are the girls? Are they there with you?'

'Don't change the subject, Ruben . . .' Loida was trying not to cry. Their two daughters were outside her room, anxiously waiting to speak to their father, but she was determined to dig deeper into the Gemma issue. She wanted him to convince her that she was worrying over nothing, that it was all in her paranoid mind. To tell the truth, she was willing to accept any decent excuse just so she could get rid of the heaviness spreading across her chest. She may not have realized it then, but she had decided long before the phone call that the only way for her to cope was to embrace denial.

'Loida, listen. I will talk to Gemma and tell her to remove those photos—'

A knock on the door cut him off, and their eldest, Jennie, poked her head in.

'Mama, can we talk to Papa now?'

That was the last time she ever heard from him. She received his remittance just as he had promised a few days after the call. And then there was nothing. He stopped sending money and stopped answering her calls. He also deactivated his Facebook account.

Frantic and desperate, Loida tried searching Gemma's profile again only to find out that she had changed her settings and blocked Loida from looking at her pictures or leaving any message. She spent the next few weeks in a hysterical cycle, vacillating between acceptance and denial. After exhausting and failing at different ways to get in touch with him in Dubai, she eventually gave up and allowed herself to crack open and disintegrate into a million pieces. It was her daughters who helped her feel whole again. Her daughters who reminded her that she still had love in her life.

'And now we're engaged!' Gemma beamed. Loida had been so caught up in her own recollection that she had not realized the moment Gemma had started babbling about her own version of how her love story with Ruben unfolded. The sound of the word 'engaged' brought Loida back to the room, where its resonance felt like tiny, twisting shrapnel embedded deep in her heart.

The pieces had scattered and wedged there, like shrapnel after a bomb explosion. A bomb that Gemma had thrown her way just a few days ago, when she had announced her happy news to the ladies at the salon. The reaction was immediate. All the other beauty therapists rushed to her, chattering like birds and cooing dramatically at the jewelled ring on her finger.

Meanwhile, Loida had to excuse herself to the ladies' toilet where she muffled her screams with a towel inside a stall. The ladies were still fawning around Gemma when Loida came back. Sick with outrage, she had asked to be let go for the rest of the day with the convincing excuse that her lunch had given her a sudden and severe case of diarrhoea.

When she had finally reached her accommodation, she had quickly dug into her luggage and took out a small, clear glass jar. She opened the metal screw top with tiny holes and held the rim to her mouth as if she was about to relieve an unquenchable thirst.

Then, in muted, angry whispers, she had unloaded all her pain and hate on the small brown beetle resting at the bottom of the jar.

The creature had stayed in one spot, twitching its wings occasionally as it listened to her whisper all the exquisite pain she wanted to inflict on Gemma and Ruben.

When she had finished, she opened her mouth, tipped the jar up and waited as the beetle crawled its way past her lips and down her throat. The toll it took on her body soon after surprised Loida. She couldn't get out of bed for a week. She should have known. This was part of the punishment she had to endure for practicing her true power.

All this time she'd held on to the idea that she was just an albularyo with special abilities but now, after this, she had to own up to it. She was a witch, a Mambabarang as the locals back home would call her kind. She had felt terrified of fully embracing this aspect of her craft before because she had known it would ask too much of her, more than she had been prepared to give. This time, however, she was willing to take the risk. Her pain was too immense, and it needed a sacrifice just as considerable.

She thought of the countless men and women who had come to her in the past, seeking relief from the paralysis of their own hate and heartache. Back then, she knew nothing of their anguish. She understood now that in the face of unforgivable betrayal and pain, what she had concocted for them were but paltry potions and spells. Mere placebos meant to make them feel as if they had power over the hurt, power over the person who had hurt them. 'Time is a great healer,' she had thought back then. Now, however, she would discover that retribution felt much better, and time was nothing but salt on a fresh, open wound.

By the time Loida had begun to apply the wax, Gemma had her eyes fixed on the ceiling. The girl had this treatment done so many times that she knew just when to relax. She took this opportunity to talk about her wedding plans. This time, she blathered on and on about whether she'd look better in a sexy or a sweet bridal gown.

If she had paid more attention, perhaps she would have noticed that Loida had turned away to let a brown beetle crawl out of her mouth. It fluttered on top of the hardening wax that Loida had just applied on Gemma's labia and waited there like a trained little pet.

'I have just this one last bit and then I'll move to the less delicate hairs, okay?' Loida said, looking up from between Gemma's legs.

'Uh-huh.' Gemma nodded without looking down, still lost in thoughts of wedding flowers and cakes.

As Loida ripped the wax off swiftly, the bug jumped to the middle of Gemma's clit and crawled halfway inside her glistening folds.

'You have some smaller hairs closer to the lip. You want to me to tweeze them off?'

'Yes, everything . . . I want it smooth and clean, please.'

Loida smiled. 'As you wish,' she said quietly and bent down closer with a pair of tweezers. She watched with satisfaction as the bug made its way inside Gemma, syncing its move with every plucking action she made with the tweezers. By the time she had cleared the area of unwanted hair, the bug had wedged the last of its dotted fluttering wings completely inside Gemma's clit.

'There, it's clean!' Loida announced. 'Now, do you want me to shape your front pubes?'

Gemma gasped. 'Oh! Can you make a heart?'

Loida couldn't help but laugh at the absurdity of her request. 'Of course,' she agreed and started working on the shape Gemma had asked for.

She almost wished that she could be there to witness the look on Ruben's face when the beetle would begin it's terrifying work on Gemma. To see the horror in his eyes as it slowly devoured his lover alive and then to realize that the monstrosity he was witnessing could only be the handiwork of one person. The only person he knew with the skill and the capability to inflict this kind of nightmare.

Loida wanted him to start thinking of her once the terror and helplessness would begin to dawn on him and take hold. She wanted him to remember her when the panic would set in, and so did the realization that the agonizing, gruesome torment Gemma was experiencing would happen to him too. Sooner or later.

When this happened, he'd have to come home, and when he did, Loida would be able to finally ease the pain that'd been eating her from inside by feeding it with his own.

'Papi will love it!' Gemma shrieked as she looked down at Loida's perfect workmanship on the pubic heart.

'Oh, I'm sure he will. I'm sure he'll be thrilled to know how much you really love him! Shall we get started on your facial now?'

'Yes, please!' Gemma clapped her hands with girlish glee and laid back down with relaxed anticipation.

Loida reached into her bag of tools and glanced at the glass jar that had once contained her beetle. Seeing it empty made her smile with satisfaction and she started pulling out the creams she would use for the facial treatment with renewed enthusiasm.

The Cook

Malta

They brought his eldest daughter to him in a black PVC bag. They called it a body bag. He'd never seen a dead body come in anything like it. It was shiny and had zippers. *So fancy*, Manoy Elmer thought. Next to him, his wife, Manay Flo, struggled to contain her despair and fell, wailing. The cameras began to whir and suddenly, the room erupted in frenetic bursts of light. There were about ten media people inside the mortuary with them. Along with a few police officers and two men in white coats. The men in white coats fascinated him. He was told they were forensic pathologists—doctors who work on dead bodies. In an alternate world, Manoy Elmer was convinced he'd have been a forensic pathologist himself. After all, he knew his way around dead bodies. Plus, he'd look good in a white lab coat, he mused and held his wife closer to him as she began to shake with grief.

It helped Manoy Elmer to think about these things now. It distracted from the powerful, overwhelming pain spreading across his heart. He refused to give in to the grief. Not yet, not now. Not while these strangers had their cameras trained on him. To fall apart now would feel like surrendering some more and he'd already surrendered enough to be in this room and this strange country, Malta. He'd never even heard of Malta until his daughter Jona announced to the family that she was striking out on her own and leaving Sorsogon to work as a cook. Of course it didn't make sense to him. They weren't well off, but they weren't exactly poor either. He'd always been able to provide with the help of the family business—a food stall he'd grown from a modest home-cooked delivery food service to a small but popular eatery at the Santa Magdalena market. They owned the land and the house they'd lived in thanks to the ancestors, their bellies were always full, and their cravings satiated.

Manoy Elmer had always made sure that his family never wanted for anything. Jona, however, constantly wanted more. She wanted a life outside of Santa Magdalena, beyond Sorsogon, away from the family and the family business. She wanted to experience the world, and she'd never made a secret of it. Among all his children, Jona was the stubbornly independent one. She was the first one to ask to be paid for the work that she did at the eatery. Something he didn't even consider until she argued that paying the children who worked at the stall would prevent them from always bothering him with every little thing they wanted for themselves. She had been right, and it wasn't until then that he realized how much time and attention all eight of his children were taking away from him, even with Manay Flo's help.

After that, he had been able to devote more time to hunting, working on new recipes, or planning the next menu. Jona was also the one to always want new clothes, new shoes, and then there was the mobile phone. She apparently needed one, desperately. But not just any mobile phone, she wanted one that took good pictures. A phone that allowed her to do things and watch things on the internet.

Manoy Elmer had never liked mobile phones because he noticed that anyone who used it while eating at his food stall seemed almost possessed by the thing. Men and women, even children, seemed hypnotized and transfixed by this tiny glowing device that prevented them from connecting with anything around them or each other. He didn't trust anything that had that much power. Especially when it was not created from the land or by the spirit. So, when he discovered that Jona finally got one that she paid for with the money she had saved working as his assistant at the eatery, Manoy Elmer knew it was only a matter of time before he would lose her to this thing too. He just never thought it would take her this far—inside a cold, brightly lit room in Malta, surrounded by cadavers.

Manoy Elmer shivered and held his sobbing wife closer, more resolute than ever to not show any emotion. He was going to be a rock for both of them, he decided even as he felt himself inching closer to falling apart as she was. No, he would save his tears and sorrow for when they finally had the room to themselves. Manoy Elmer thought of it as the only private thing he could hold on to. The only thing he had left of his dignity since he and his wife had allowed the whole world into their lives.

His defiance, however, did not last long. When they finally wheeled his two-year-old granddaughter's body inside a small black body bag in front of them, the cracks inside him widened and the dam he had so carefully built, finally collapsed. Manoy Elmer disintegrated, and he wept. The room erupted in a fervour of renewed clicks and lights and for a few agonizing moments, there was nothing but the sound of Manoy Elmer and Manay Flo wailing inconsolably. This was the first time they'd see Mary Kaye. Before waking up to this nightmare a few weeks ago, the couple had only seen her on video calls with Jona. Eventually, a female voice from the back rose with authority above the fray.

'Please! Please! Thank you everyone but let's now leave the family to grieve in private,' she said and began to make her way to the weeping couple. Manoy Elmer felt her stand close, lean over, and place her hand on his back. He heard a few more camera clicks go off before she finally spoke again. This time, she addressed them directly, her voice low and soft, almost apologetic for intruding on their public anguish.

'Manoy Elmer, Manay Flo . . . We will get rid of the press people first, okay? And then the pathologists will open the bags so you can identify your daughter and granddaughter to the police. Are you ready to do this?'

Manoy Elmer nodded but Manay Flo continued to sob into his chest. 'Thank you, Joy,' he managed to say, feeling somewhat better that they were finally getting closer to being alone with Jona and Mary Kaye.

They met Joy Wilwayco shortly after the office of Sorsogon Congressman Rogelio got involved. Weeks after their regular catch up with Jona had stopped, they got in touch with several labour government agencies and were met with nothing but delays and infuriating bureaucracy. Eventually, they decided to make their plight known on social media in the hopes that someone would come forward with information or assistance. By chance, the story was picked up by local media and they were approached for an interview on Albay Radio. It wasn't an easy decision for the family. However, as more days dragged on without any news from Jona, they began to feel desperate and hopeless. They had no choice but to allow strangers into their life. So, they agreed to be interviewed.

Joy showed up at their home unannounced soon after and invited them to the city hall to talk to the congressman about their situation. In a way, it was an ambush. The Congressman made a beeline for Manoy Elmer and Manay Flo as soon as they arrived (along with the rest of their seven children) and made a big show of his concern and assistance for the local press people in attendance. In the end, Manoy Elmer wasn't at all surprised at the way things turned out. It was, after all, an election year and everyone knew that the ambitious congressman would do anything to get re-elected, especially since he'd hinted in the past that he'd like the opportunity to serve the country as its president.

Manoy Elmer did not like the Congressman at all. Although he'd never voted and never involved himself in anything related to Sorsogon politics, he was aware that Rogelio was as corrupt as they came. At least according to most people who come to dine at his eatery. Besides, there was something about the way the Congressman smelled that made him feel unsettled. Like the way he could tell if something about the meat was off, no matter how good or fresh it looked on display. During this meeting, the Congressman personally appointed Joy as the family chaperone. A kind of caretaker for the family to guide them through this unthinkable ordeal.

'Think of her as an extension of me,' he remembered the Congressman saying to him and his wife. 'Everything you need, Joy will take care of it for you. Just don't forget to mention my name every now and then when the media is around, okay?' he said, squeezing Manoy Elmer's shoulders before turning to the cameras and pulling him closer as if he'd been part of their family all along.

Things moved quickly after that. The office of Foreign Affairs eventually got involved and mobilized the Philippine consul in Valletta to pressure the local police into investigating Jona and Mary Kaye's disappearance. The next time Joy had come to visit them at the house, Manoy Elmer had known something was very wrong.

She sat them down with a very grave look on her face and apologized immediately for the news she was about to give them. Even before Joy finished saying the words—that the Valletta police had found Jona's body, Manay Flo had started to cry. Manoy Elmer, for his part, refused to believe. For him, it was simply unthinkable.

While the rest of the children gathered around Manay Flo, he pushed Joy for more information about what had happened, in the hopes that she'd say something that would invalidate the awful truth. But each detail that came out of her mouth was an unmistakable confirmation that Jona was gone. In the midst of the anguished wailing around him, Joy revealed to Manoy Elmer that according to the Valletta police, Jona's body had been found stuffed inside a large suitcase that was left at the city bus depot.

'And our apo, Mary Kaye? Do they have any news about her?' Manay Flo managed to interject. The house fell quiet, and Joy shook her head before saying, 'No.'

Manay Flo looked with hopeful eyes at Manoy Elmer before saying, 'She could still be alive, right?'

He didn't know what to say. He'd yet to get over the image of Jona's body folded inside a bag like an unwanted piece of clothing. Before she had left for Malta, Jona had assured him that she'd take every precaution to be safe. She had promised him she won't be stupid, she had promised him that she'd be okay. That was three years ago. After a year of living in Malta without an incident, he started to feel assured that perhaps Jona was going to be okay after all. Even after she'd shocked the family with the news that she was pregnant and was going to keep the baby. Manoy Elmer (after a considerable time) trusted her—albeit questionable—decision. Perhaps most challenging of all was accepting that she was going to raise this child without the support of the married man who got her pregnant.

Despite their best efforts to convince her to come home, she had decided to stay in Malta and somehow managed to make it work. She was resilient that way. She was also infuriatingly stubborn that way. Nevertheless, it didn't stop him and Manay Flo from constantly asking her to reconsider her plans. It just didn't feel right that she wasn't back home raising this child. But, most of all, it felt wrong that their first grandchild would not receive the blessing of their ancestors. As with everyone in the family, she must go through the sacred rites, even if Jona would prefer to deny their customs. There was no denying nature. Mary Kaye belonged with them in Santa Magdalena even if half of her was Italian.

It made Manoy Elmer wonder, *Is it possible that whoever got her pregnant could somehow be involved in her death?* She never did tell them much about him. They only knew that Jona had met him online, he was Italian, and he worked as a banker in the city. During one of their past video chats, she even referred to him as 'the one'. It annoyed him now that he could not even remember his name.

'Who did this to her Joy? Do they know?' he asked.

The whole family turned to Joy, eager to get answers. 'The police don't know yet. The only thing they know is that there are more victims. I mean they're still finding more as we speak. They think it might be the work of a serial killer.'

Manoy Elmer had never heard of such a thing. 'What is a serial killer? I don't understand.'

'Someone who kills more than one person, often murdering his victims in the same way. People like this, sometimes they will keep on killing until they get caught.' Joy suddenly became very reflective. 'I hope they catch whoever did this soon. He's the only person who can tell us where to find Mary Kaye.'

Jona knows, Manoy Elmer thought with certainty. They were going to get the answers they needed. They just had to do it very, very soon.

'Joy, where is Jona's body now? And do you think you can help take us to where she is?' Manoy Elmer asked with urgency.

When they landed in Valletta two days later, they received the heartbreaking news that Mary Kaye's body had been found in a lake south-west of the city. Her decomposing remains were inside a bag, wrapped in bed sheets and tied by a rope to a cement block. Eventually, it was also revealed that a total of ten other bodies had been found. Three of the victims were Filipinas, the rest were of different nationalities. There was also a Russian woman and a Sri Lankan woman among the victims. Worse yet, the body of another child was also found. She had been stuffed inside a suitcase with her presumed mother. Upon further investigation by the police, it was also revealed that almost all of the adult victims had been working as housekeepers.

By the time Manoy Elmer and Manay Flo reached the doorstep of Valletta General Hospital where the morgue was located, the international press interest and coverage was at a fever pitch. Given the intense attention the case was generating, it hadn't been surprising how quickly Congressman Rogelio agreed to finance their trip. The media crush at the Manila airport where he personally escorted Manoy Elmer and his wife provided the perfect platform for the Congressman to beef up his image some more and ingratiate himself to a wider audience. Not that Manoy Elmer minded, what mattered more then was that they get to Jona as quickly as they could before it was too late. If it meant standing next to an openly corrupt politician and directly acknowledging him for his part in reuniting them with their deceased daughter, so be it. Besides that was the easy part.

Before getting on the twenty-two-hour flight from Manila to Malta, the couple had never been on a plane before. They had never left Santa Magdalena, ever. To do so required the permission of the ancestors so that they could do what they needed to do. At the family temple in Santa Magdalena, Manoy Elmer and Manay Flo offered an unscheduled sacrifice so that they could take one of their sacred relics with them—the skin of their great, great grandfather encased in a small jar dangling at the end of intricately carved devotional beads. It looked similar to a Catholic rosary. They had never taken any of the sacred family relics out of Santa Magdalena before but Jona's death in Malta had forced their hand. Extraordinary circumstances required extraordinary action. It hadn't even occurred to Manoy Elmer that what they were about to do may not work. Why wouldn't it? The power of the ancestors had never failed them before. For Manoy Elmer and Manay Flo, there was no reason to believe that it would fail them now, especially when it involved assisting a descendant.

Manoy Elmer continued to think about the implications of what they were about to attempt as he watched the press people begin to file out of the morgue with the assistance of the Valletta police. Then, the men in white lab coats moved to stand closer to the bodies of his daughter and granddaughter lying on top of the steel autopsy table in front of them. Manoy Elmer dreaded the silence of the room.

'Are you ready for us to open the bags?' Manoy Elmer heard one of the men in white lab coats ask.

He felt Manay Flo tighten in his embrace. Joy looked at both for them for consent.

'Are you ready to see Jona and Mary Kaye, Flo?' Manoy Elmer asked, holding her closer. 'You know we have to do this,' he added, more to himself than to his sobbing wife.

Manay Flo nodded her head and hesitantly straightened up without saying a word.

Manoy Elmer nodded at Joy.

'Yes, they're ready,' Joy said to the men.

'First we'll have you identify the adult victim . . .'

When they unzipped the bag containing Jona's body, Manoy Elmer's stomach lurched. Not because the smell of the decomposition was overwhelming but because he could smell the powerful solution they had used to preserve her body. For him, this was a disappointing development and would make their task that much more challenging. The doctors stopped short of completely opening the bag, revealing only Jona's head.

Manay Flo's weeping filled the room once more.

'Is this your daughter?' one of the police officers asked. 'Can you confirm that this is Jona Mae Buluag?'

He wished more than anything that he could say no. To say out loud and with certainty, 'This is not my daughter at all. This is not Jona. This has all been a big mistake. She's not this pallid, decomposing cadaver with white, glassy open eyes. This is not her, my daughter's not dead.' Tears began to fall from his eyes, and he found himself nodding his head.

'Jona,' he heard Manay Flo call out to her as if she was going to wake up from her deceased rest. Then, she tearfully moved to cradle Jona's head inside the body bag. The men in white lab coats respectfully gave her the space and allowed them a few more minutes of grieving before they turned to Mary Kaye's body bag next to Jona's.

'Wait,' Manoy Elmer interrupted. 'What happened to my daughter? How did she die?' Manoy Elmer turned to the police.

'Based on their initial examination . . .' Joy began translating for Manoy Elmer as one of the men in white lab coats began to speak. 'She died by strangulation. Though they can't officially say with finality that this is the absolute cause of her death without a full and complete examination.'

Suddenly, Manoy Elmer began to feel weak and did not realize that he must have needed support because unexpectedly, he felt Joy's hands grab his shoulders to support him.

'Manoy?' he heard her say. 'Are you okay? We can stop, you know. They have given us all the time you'll need to do this.' He noticed that her voice sounded muffled before observing that she was covering her nose and mouth with a medicated rag. Considering the overpowering smell of the dead in the room, he was impressed that she hasn't excused herself to leave or throw up. Suddenly, Manay Flo reached for his hands and stood next to him. 'Elmer, I don't know if I'm ready to see Mary Kaye,' she said still crying.

The man in the white lab coat moved to open the other bag containing their grandchild. As soon as he unzipped the bag to reveal the tiny head of a toddler, a stronger, more powerful smell of decomposition began to fill the room. It was finally too much for Joy. She managed to blurt out an 'excuse me' before bolting for the toilet.

The police and the doctors, however, were unfazed. 'Is this your grandchild? Is this Mary Kaye Buluag?' The man in the white lab coat directed his question at Manoy Elmer and Manay Flo.

They answered with profound grief. The couple began to wail. They both collapsed on the floor, weighed down by the gravity of their pain. The doctors and the police stood in silent witness of their grief, unsure of what to do and at a complete loss of what to say in the face of such devastating tragedy. The couple was still crumpled on the floor when Joy finally emerged from the bathroom. She rushed to them with her arms wide open and stayed with them on the floor before, eventually, helping both of them up.

Before Manoy Elmer could even ask the question, one of the men in white coats began to talk. 'Our initial observation of the child's body also suggests strangulation but as we've mentioned earlier, we'll know for sure what caused her death only after a full autopsy.'

Manoy Elmer collected himself enough to ask, 'Joy, can you also find out how much they've done on Jona's body? Have they removed everything inside?'

Joy turned to the group and asked the men the question in English. The men in white lab coats confirmed that they had left Jona's body untouched after the initial forensic examination as requested by the family. With regards to Mary Kaye, they added that since her body had just been found, they hadn't gone through the process of preserving her body. She had undergone a regular external forensic examination and the police had taken photographs for the investigation but nothing apart from that.

'We understand that the parents want to grieve with the bodies of their loved ones according to the customs of the family,' one of the police officers addressed Joy. 'But can you help us understand exactly what's going to happen during the time we leave them alone with the bodies?'

Manoy Elmer watched Joy explain to the men in the room that the family were members of a little known indigenous community in the Philippines. And, as members of this community, they had a specific way of grieving and honouring their dead. During the hour that the family had asked to be alone with the bodies, a scaled down version of a community ceremony would be performed to prepare the bodies for transport back home. She emphasized that this was a very sacred process for them and respectfully asked everyone to give them absolute privacy and not disturb them during this time. Joy assured the officials that there would just be a lot praying and incantations, nothing more.

Most of this was not entirely a lie. Manoy Elmer came up with the story shortly after realizing that they needed to get to Jona in Malta. If he was honest about it, he wasn't entirely sure what he was doing when he came up with the story. He only knew that it had to be convincing enough for Joy to take their request to the congressman. The men asked for assurance that the couple would not touch or move the bodies in any way to preserve the integrity of the evidence and their investigation. Manoy Elmer and Manay Flo nodded in agreement and the men turned to leave when suddenly, Manoy Elmer grabbed Joy for help with one more question.

'Can you ask them about the person who did this to my family? Do they know anything about the killer yet?'

Even as Manoy Elmer could not fully understand what the police officers were saying to Joy, he speculated from the way they shook their heads and spoke carefully that they didn't have the answer to his question. And if they didn't have the answer, how could they possibly catch the monster who took Jona and Mary Kaye away from them? He decided that the police needed their help, and he began to feel a little more confident about what they were about to do some more. He thought back to what Joy had said to them in Sorsogon and how people like that would keep on killing until they were caught. *Will there be more victims? Not if we can help it,* Manoy Elmer thought with a simmering sense of retribution

Joy turned to them after talking to the police. 'Manoy Elmer . . . Manay Flo . . . the police said that they are following a few leads but since it's an ongoing investigation, it's too early to share any information at the moment.'

'It's okay, we'll find out soon enough,' Manay Flo said absently. Joy gave her a surprised look.

'How do you mean?' she asked.

'Manay meant that she can't wait to find out from the police soon enough,' Manoy Elmer interrupted and shot Manay a stern look.

'Yes!' Manay quickly tried to correct herself. 'I meant I can't wait to find out from the police and yes, I hope it happens soon.'

After everyone else had left the room, Manoy Elmer stood by the door to make sure no one was standing outside, listening in. It was only after he was confident they had complete privacy that he began to walk back to Manay Flo who was standing next to the bodies. He glared at her.

'I can't believe you said what you did earlier. You nearly gave me a heart attack there,' he said, more annoyed than he realized.

'Eh,' she grunted as she reached inside the bag she had carried into the morgue with her.

'You worry too much!' she continued. 'These people are too clueless to know what we are going to do here.'

As she unpacked her bag, Manoy Elmer unzipped the body bags completely. The full sight of Jona and Mary Kaye's decomposing bodies stunned them into silence. Not so much because they were taken aback by the woeful condition of the bodies but because they could feel the pain they had suffered. Pain radiated from every tortured sinew in their contorted and distended flesh. Soon, Manoy Elmer and Manay Flo would feel their suffering too. Without realizing it, the couple began to transform.

Back in Sorsogon, some people would call them Anduduno, but most would likely refer to them as Aswang na Lakaw, the Walking Aswang—ghouls that feed on the flesh of the dead. While most of their kind had moved deeper into the mountains and forests of Mt Bulusan, the Buluag clan had thrived in Santa Magdalena. A modest quiet town along the coastline that used to be their ancestors home base for centuries. It used to be remote and unknown, the perfect home for a community of Andudunos, a safe place they could retreat to after feeding and exist with their families in peace. But that had been a long time ago. That Santa Magdalena now only existed in fairy tales passed down by their ancestors. How the Buluag managed to remain and become part of the community was largely due to the handiwork of their great grandfather, Manoy Fred.

The way Manoy Fred looked at it, they were there before anyone else, so why should they move? It helped that he had a great talent for cooking, and he used this skill to ensure their survival in Santa Magdalena. While most Andudunos were content eating corpses fresh from the grave, Manoy Fred took cadaver pieces home and experimented with them.

Enhancing decomposing human flesh, bones, and tendons with local ingredients to make delectable versions of Bicolano favourites. Feeding his family this way eliminated the need for them to prowl around cemeteries or hunt sick people. It allowed them to control and hide their transformations and gave them the flexibility to grow their kind. More importantly, it allowed them to continue worshipping their ancestors and practise their craft, which, in large part, they used to cast a kind of spell on Santa Magdalena. An enchantment, so to speak, through food.

From Kandingga, Kinunot, to Bicol Express, Manoy Fred had cooked with measured pieces of seasoned cadavers and shared his dishes with the neighbourhood. Everyone loved them and everyone wanted more. Soon enough, he began making a living out of his cooking. After that, it only made sense that he'd pass on his skills and recipes to his descendants to ensure the survival of their kind. Manoy Elmer was the one who decided to eventually open a food stall after much convincing from customers who could not get enough of his cooking. Manoy Elmer was never one to brag but he was convinced that his cooking was better than everyone else's in the family. They were doing so well that Jona even suggested they should open another branch in Albay and volunteered to manage it if he agreed. He should have realized then that this was one her earlier attempts to get away from the family.

Manoy Elmer and Manay Flo looked at each other in their Anduduno form and sighed with relief. This was the longest they'd had to be in human form. With all that they had to endure to get there, the sight of their clawed hands and the feel of their fangs through their snouts was a welcome change. It made them feel at home even when they were in such unfamiliar surroundings.

'Let's get started,' Manoy Elmer said and laid down his favourite cutting knife next to the items Manay Flo had laid out near Jona's body. Next to it were a few other items they had taken with them from home, which included a piece of bark from a tree in Santa Magdalena that would allow them to summon the power of their ancestors. It was a necessary part of their ritual, since they could not do anything without a natural anchor that tied them to the land of Sorsogon and without the family prayer beads.

'We're going to have to start with the brain, Elmer. It will give us better vision. I just hope the formaldehyde hasn't affected the meat too much. I don't want to have to eat Mary Kaye unless we absolutely have to,' Manay Flo said as she began to crush some of the prayer beads with her hands against the autopsy table. 'That means we'll have to borrow their bone saw.'

Manoy Elmer understood and walked over to one of the steel trays holding some postmortem equipment. He had spied it earlier when they walked in. Fortunately for them, one of the equipment laid out was a surgical saw. He grabbed it and walked back to the bodies.

Manay Flo began the incantation as soon as Manoy Elmer took his position next to her. They laid their hands over the items and began to pray in unison.

'Mighty Lord Asuang source of all life, we stand before you with reverence and humility. We seek the blessing of your divine power. Oh great father, breathe your spell into these objects, make them a conduit, a tool to carry out your mighty work. Let us divine through your will and through the sacred flesh of your faithful what has come before. Grant us the justice and retribution we seek, Amen'

Manoy Elmer didn't waste any time. The word 'amen', had barely left his lips when he grabbed his cutting knife and began to carefully cut around the top of Jona's head. After he had sliced through the area with confident precision, he yanked her scalp off by her hair. Then, he took the bone saw and started working on removing the top of Jona's skull. Meanwhile, Manay Flo continued to pray over the sound of steady grinding. The whole process took minutes. When Manoy Elmer finished, he carefully laid the top of her skull to the side along with her scalp, grabbed his cutting knife, and cut out a piece of her brain. He handed it to Manay Flo, who held it in one claw as if it was the most precious thing she'd ever held. Then, she uttered a short prayer to call on the spirit of Manoy Fred before using her claw to scoop some of his ground bones from the prayer beads and sprinkle it on top of Jona's brain. 'Guide us now,' she said, ending the prayer.

Manoy Elmer took the piece of Jona's brain from Manay Flo's hand and sliced it into two. They each took a piece and ate their way into their daughter's final memories.

The last twenty-four hours. That's what they'd get of Jona's last few moments. It had always been this way, and they had never questioned why. They were not sure what they'd get to see but from what they remembered, they knew they would only get fragments of her memories and only the memories that were significant enough to leave an imprint on her anatomy. No matter. They only needed to see the face the man who did this to their family, perhaps figure out where he was and then let the police know.

How they would explain themselves to the authorities and to Joy after all this was something they didn't want to focus on right now. They had to find this killer and soon. Right now, they were just grateful and relieved that their ancestor's power was strong enough to cross continents and guide them. The couple faced each other and held hands. Holding on to each other not just for support but to share the pain of what they were about to witness.

Dead divination was a craft few Anduduno's practice. Mostly because doing so reminded them of the humanity of what they were about to consume. An experience that interfered with the pleasure of enjoying their meal. Especially when, almost always, the first memory they encountered was the person's moment of death. Jona's memories opened themselves to Manoy Elmer first. His body shook and he started to choke. Manay Flo began to see and experience things soon after. While performing dead divination, they would see and experience the same thing, but what they perceived would depend on how observant they were.

'He's killing her,' Manay Flo cried and just like Manoy Elmer was, she also began to choke. The couple held on to each other tighter and allowed the agony of their daughter's death to pass through them.

'Oh Jona . . .' Manoy Elmer cried out. Tears flowed down his cheeks.

They began to see through her eyes, but what they saw wouldn't make complete sense until after the moment of death. Until then, the vision was blurry, like they were watching events unfold from under murky water. A few minutes later, they still could not get a clear picture of her killer. At one point, they saw Jona's hands clawing at the killer's face. She had fought. Or at least tried to.

'I can't see him, Elmer. Can you?'

'Not yet . . .'

Suddenly, the sensation of pain shifted from agonizing hurt to pleasure. Manay Flo was the first to express her confusion.

'What's happening?'

Manoy Elmer, however, immediately understood but didn't quite know what to say to his wife. The sensation of experiencing Jona's intimate time with this man was uncomfortable but he hoped that maybe this moment of passion would finally reveal the man's face to them.

'Just concentrate on his face, Flo,' he said.

Manay Flo started to moan in response to what she was experiencing. Her body began to arch and writhe. Manoy Elmer kept quiet. He felt the sensation of Jona's pleasure too. But, as a mother, it made sense that Manay Flo would feel Jona's emotions more intensely.

Manoy Elmer tried to ignore the bizarre mix of pleasure and discomfort he was feeling by focusing on seeing the face of the killer. He waited but as more time passed, he began to feel frustrated as the vision wasn't giving them a clear picture of the killer at all. Finally, Manay Flo spoke again.

'It's the formaldehyde. It's affecting the quality of the vision.'

The couple needed to make a decision and Manoy Elmer was suddenly worried that they don't have enough time.

'Maybe her heart will give us a clearer vision?' Manay Flo suggested, sensing his frustration.

Getting a piece of Jona's heart was something that Manoy Elmer would rather not do. Even if, as an Anduduno, he possessed the strength and the skill to easily open her chest cavity, it would take too much time and worse, it would be too messy. He refused to desecrate her body any more than they had to. Explaining the opened skull to the police and the men in white lab coats was going to be challenging enough. Also, consuming a piece of her heart wasn't a guarantee of a better vision. If the brain was no good, chances were, the heart wouldn't be either. They might have to eat a piece of Mary Kaye.

'I don't know if I can survive feeling her pain, Elmer,' Manay Flo said mournfully.

He held her close once more and said, 'We have no choice and we're running out of time.'

The couple turned to the tiny body in front of them and repeated the same ceremony of invocation. Except, this time, Manay Flo cried throughout the whole ordeal. She was still crying when they finally sat down and began to chew a piece of their grandchild's brain.

Manoy Elmer kept it together until the moment Mary Kaye's death came to both of them. In contrast to the visions from Jona's brain, Mary Kaye's vision was vivid and detailed. The couple wept as they laboured to breathe. Unlike Jona, Mary Kaye had not struggled. She was too young to know what was happening at that moment. It was then that they came face-to-face with the killer. His hands were around her neck, squeezing as he watched her young life slowly leave her tiny body. He killed her with a chilling calm that suggested he would have no problem doing this again and again. He almost seemed bored. Manoy Elmer felt his anger rising.

'Can you see him, Flo?' he asked his wife.

'Yes,' she said crying. 'I see the monster.'

The couple focused on every detail of his face. The thinning dark hair, the deep-set eyes. He had thick, bushy brows and a handsome slender nose. They also noticed a mole on his chin. Manoy Elmer and Manay Flo were still focused on memorizing the killer's face when the vision changed. Unexpectedly, Jona came into view and the couple were overcome with a euphoric joy that surprised them.

They knew then, they were feeling Mary Kaye's joy at the presence of her mother. The couple started to cry again. This time, they wept tears of joy. They wept with the happiness of seeing Jona alive. The vision brightened some more and showed them Jona hugging and kissing Mary Kaye, both unaware of the danger they were facing. Manoy Elmer and Manay Flo suddenly wished they could stay in that vision forever. It looked and felt so real. They wanted to stop time and step into that memory, to hold both of them and take them back home. They ached over the helplessness they felt because of the inevitable brutality that awaited the mother and daughter. But as the vision continued to show Jona and Mary Kaye laughing and full of life, their hearts began to heal. Even if just for a little.

Tearfully, the couple thanked their ancestors for granting them the grace of seeing mother and daughter this way. For allowing them to remember the love they had for each other and providing a bit of reprieve from the relentless tide of despair.

Then, as if the ancestors were reminding the couple of the important task they had set out to do, the couple started to feel unsettled once more and the killer came into view again. The sight of him in a policeman's uniform made them gasp. He walked into the room where Jona and Mary Kaye were staying, and the feeling of dread returned tenfold.

Mary Kaye knew. The child somehow sensed the evil in this man, and she began to cry. Manoy Elmer and Manay Flo watched Jona place Mary Kaye back in her crib and rush over to the killer with a kiss, excitedly calling out his name as she did so.

'Matteo! You're home!' Jona exclaimed.

'Matteo!' Manoy Elmer and Many Flo exclaimed together. In an instant, the vision ended.

Overcome with relief, Manoy Elmer and Manay Flo pulled each other close and held one another for a few quiet minutes.

'It's over,' Manay Flo said. The exhaustion of what they'd just had to endure suddenly hit her.

Manoy Elmer nodded, but he knew better. It was just beginning. With the killer clearly being a police officer, they couldn't trust the authorities. If only the ancestors could tell them what to do next.

Moments later, they began to tidy up. They put away the beads, the knife, and zipped up the body bags to reveal only Jona and Mary Kaye's head as before. Then, they stood in front of the bodies for one final prayer of thanks to the ancestors. They also used this time to focus their will on hiding their Andudono form.

Manoy Elmer looked at the big clock hanging on a wall inside the morgue and saw that they still had a few minutes before they needed to open the door. He looked at Manay Flo. 'Are you ready?' She gave him a brave smile in response and nodded. They both walked up to the morgue door and opened it.

Glossary

The creatures of *The Secret Lives of OFWs*

ALBULARYO: A term that comes from the Spanish *herbolario*, meaning herbalist. Albularyos can be all sorts of healers, from folk practitioners to medicine men or even witch doctors. They are oftentimes found in the countryside, using herbs and traditional methods like *hilot* or massage to help people feel better. Depending on the region, they are either considered to be the first option for healing right off the bat, while others might only turn to them as a last resort. In pre-Spanish-colonized Philippines, albularyos were what we'd call *Babaylans* or *Catalonans*. These were like the OG healers, on the same level as the village leaders or *datus*. Pre-colonial Filipinos believed these Babaylans could communicate with spirits in nature, doing everything from influencing the weather to curing the sick and keeping curses at bay.

In modern times, belief in the efficacy of albularyos has waned, yet there remain adherents to the practice of folk medicine. It is worth noting, however, that some albularyos reputedly engage in practices involving black magic, purportedly possessing the ability to cast curses on individuals. The majority of albularyos adhere to traditional methods, utilizing prayers or incantations known as '*orasyon*' during their rituals. In the pursuit of medicinal plants, referred to as *pangalap*, they collect various plant parts including leaves, barks, roots, and oils such as coconut oil, which they combine in a process known as *pabukal* to create remedies. This process may involve the addition of their saliva or the use of special writing on paper. Additionally, some practitioners employ crystals or *tawas* for diagnosis while others utilize candle wax, eggs, or spiritual guidance for divination purposes. When patients suspect their ailment is caused by supernatural beings like *Lamang Lupa* or *Engkantos*, albularyos employ a combination of rituals and prayers to expel these spirits and alleviate the illness.

ANDUDUNO: According to Bicolano folklore, the Anduduno is an aswang with the ability to detect terminal illness through scent. It lurks outside or beneath the victim's house, utilizing its lengthy, serpentine tongue to lick the sick individual until their demise. On occasion, it waits near the residence of a terminally ill person and, upon their burial, exhumes the body to consume the corpse. In this anthology, the Anduduno is a form of a ghoul. In Maximo Ramos' *The Aswang Complex in Philippine Folklore* the Philippine ghoul is said to steal human corpses and devour them. It's described as having horns and curved, sharp nails with pointed teeth. Its smell is fetid and though generally invisible, the creature is said to look like a human being when it shows itself. According to Ramos' book, some ghouls live in human communities. At night, they congregate in large trees near a cemetery and then descend and exhume the newly buried corpses. A ghoul is said to be able to hear the groans of the dying over a great distance. Its greed is aroused when it catches the scent of the death, and then it snatches the mourners as well as the dead.

ASWANG NA LAYOG: The *Aswang Na Layog*, translated from Bicolano as 'Flying Aswang', is a subtype of the aswang, akin to the Manananggal. This classification was first mentioned in a book published in 1949 titled *An mga Asuwang: A Bicol Belief* by Father Frank Lynch, an American scholar and Jesuit professor of Anthropology and Sociology at Ateneo de Manila University. Father Frank's study served as the foundation for subsequent works on aswang mythology, including *The Aswang Inquiry* by GCF and *The Aswang Complex in Philippine Folklore* by Maximo Ramos. In his research, Father Frank delineates two types of aswang: the Aswang na Layog and the Manananggal. While the Manananggal is widely known for leaving its torso and limbs behind while its head and entrails fly away, the Aswang na Layog is known for flying with its whole body intact.

ASWANG NA LAKAW: The *Aswang na Lakaw* or translated in English as the 'Walking Aswang', is a subtype of aswang elaborated upon by Francis Lynch in his work *An Mga Asuwang: A Bicol Belief.* This particular type of aswang is the most prevalent. An Aswang na Lakaw typically commences its nightly activities around 6 p.m. by either placing its ear to a rice mortar to listen for sounds of mourning or by standing on its head and listening for such sounds. Alternatively, it may rest in a shallow hole in the ground, where some believe it removes the cover of a specially crafted listening device to eavesdrop. Then, it sets out for its nocturnal operations. Some accounts suggest that this aswang applies a unique concoction to its body, a pre-prepared ointment made from a mixture of chicken dung and coconut oil.

ASUANG/ASWANG: The earliest documentation of the aswang dates back to the sixteenth century, where it was mentioned by Spanish missionary Juan de Placensia in his work *Customs of the Tagalog*. In this text, the term aswang, spelled 'Osuang', was interpreted to mean sorcerer. Subsequently, in 1909, Isabelo de los Reyes published a book titled *La Religion Antigua de los Filipinos*, suggesting that the word aswang was derived from the Sanskrit term '*asura*', signifying demons or, more specifically, power-seeking demons. However, there is also a belief among some that it originated from the Tagalog word 'aso', meaning 'dog', possibly due to the creatures often taking the form of dogs.

Because of many conflicting interpretations, Philippine folklore expert Maximo Ramos suggested that the term 'aswang' eventually evolved into an umbrella term for various Filipino supernatural beings. According to Ramos, these beings can be categorized into five groups, which parallel creatures from Western traditions: the vampire, the self-segmenting viscera sucker, the weredog, the witch, and the ghoul. In the context of anthropology, the aswang emerged from Philippine folklore with stories dating back to at least the sixteenth century, when Spanish explorers documented the first written record of the creature. Father Frank Lynch, in his book *An Mga Asuang:*

Bicol Belief, noted however that among all the monsters in Filipino folklore, the aswang was the most feared by native people. In many contemporary retellings of aswang lore, it is believed that being an aswang is hereditary. If someone comes from a family of aswangs, they are likely to inherit the curse and develop a craving for human flesh. In some tales, the transformation into an aswang involves passing a black chick from the mouth of a dying aswang to its immediate heir. Until this ritual is completed, the aswang cannot die naturally. Known as expert shapeshifters, aswangs can seamlessly disguise themselves as humans or animals at will.

BAKUNAWA: Bakunawa is a serpent-like dragon from Philippine mythology that is known to cause eclipses, earthquakes, rain, and wind. While it is commonly depicted as a sea serpent, there are also sources referencing that it resides in the sky or the underworld. The term 'Bakunawa' is thought to originate from a compound word meaning 'bent snake'. According to folklore, the movements of the Bakunawa serve as a geomantic calendar system utilized by ancient Filipinos in divination rituals conducted by babaylan shamans. These pre-colonial shamans would typically be women healers but sometimes would identify as transgender or gender fluid. In Bicol and Visayas folklore, the Bakunawa serves as a guardian of the passage to the underworld. However, perceptions of the Bakunawa differ between the two regions. In Visayas, it is regarded as a malevolent deity associated with bad luck and misfortune. Conversely, in Bicol, the Bakunawa was initially seen as a benevolent deity before facing punishment from the supreme deity. In Bicolano myths, she was revered as the most beautiful and powerful Naga, eventually ascending to the status of a goddess and the guardian of the passage to the underworld.

BALYANA: In Bicolano lore, balyanas are like the wise women of an ancient Bicol tribe. They believe in an afterworld ruled by powerful deities like Gugurang and Asuang, benevolent and vengeful gods who control nature and life itself. Balyanas are known for being sharp and charming. Additionally, they not only lead tribal ceremonies but also hear out the tribe's problems and ask the anitos, or spirits, for advice on what to do when faced with problems in life.

ENGKANTO: Engkanto, deriving from the Spanish word for 'enchantment', serve as a broad term encompassing various mythical creatures from Philippine folklore. The term was introduced by the Spanish, who encountered a diverse array of mythical creatures in the Philippines and labelled them collectively as 'the Enchanted'. Engkantos are depicted as mystical spirits tied to nature, capable of assuming human forms. They're often likened to sirens, dark entities, and elves, exhibiting traits similar to humans, such as susceptibility to illness and mortality. Their appearances vary widely, ranging from beautiful beings to those with unique features like high-bridged noses and no philtrum (the vertical indention on the upper lip).

According to folklore, Engkantos often reside in natural surroundings, appearing as large rocks, trees, or even shadowy human forms. These mystical beings prefer to inhabit in nature, particularly in large trees like the balete, where they store their belongings. On occasion, they may choose to reside with a human, often when the individual is in a trance or experiencing extreme fatigue. Engkantos are said to exhibit both benevolent and malevolent tendencies. While some stories depict them as bestowing great fortune upon favoured individuals, others highlight their harmful effects.

Those who incur their displeasure may experience depression, madness, or even prolonged disappearances, possibly due to possession. Additionally, Engkantos are believed to cause fevers, skin ailments and may lead travellers astray or even abduct them. To prevent the risk of encountering malevolent Engkantos, individuals often carry protective charms called '*anting-anting*' or '*agimat*'. These magical amulets serve to ward off evil spirits and safeguard the wearer from harm. However, if and when they do favour an individual, they are said to be generous and capable of providing power and riches to that person. The homes of those they befriend are known to transform into magnificent palaces. Some albularyos even believe that by communing with an Engkanto during 'holy days', they can obtain improved healing powers as well as gain the knowledge on how to effectively deal with evil spirits

MAMBABARANG: This is practitioner of dark magic called 'sympathetic magic', deeply rooted in indigenous Philippine religions. This ancient craft goes by various names across the archipelago, such as *Kulam, Gaway* (Tagalog), *Barang, Hiwit, Luga* (Visayan), *Tanem, Tamay* (Ilocano), and *Pantak* (Moro). Despite the diverse terminology, the techniques remain strikingly similar throughout the Philippine islands.

Sympathetic magic involves utilizing beetles, effigies, poppets (dolls representing individuals), boiling pots, or other symbolic representations of the intended victim.

A Mambabarang, often employs insects or spirits to infiltrate the bodies of their enemies. These individuals, often ordinary humans endowed with black magic skills, possess the ability to torment and ultimately kill their victims by infesting them with insects. In folklore, Mambabarangs are said to maintain a swarm of carnivorous beetles housed in a bottle or in bamboo, meticulously nourishing them with ginger root. When they're ready to invoke their dark craft, they engage in a prayer ritual, whispering instructions and identifying the intended victim to the beetles. These voracious beetles are then released to seek out the victim, gaining entry through any bodily opening, including the nose, mouth, ears, anus, or wounds. Depending on the point of entry, the victim experiences various manifestations of invasion, such as severe haemorrhoids if the beetle enters through the anus or ear aches if the entry was gained through the ears. The resulting affliction is said to be resistant to conventional medical treatment and only reveals its true nature when the victim dies, and the insects emerge from the body's cavities.

MANANANGGAL: Known as a viscera sucker, the name of this creature is derived from the Tagalog word *'tanggal'*, meaning 'to remove' or 'to separate' because it can detach its upper torso from its lower body. This legendary being is prominently featured in Visayan folklore, particularly in the western provinces of Capiz, Iloilo, Bohol, and Antique. Often depicted as female with vampiric traits, it possesses the ability to sever its upper body and sprout enormous bat-like wings, enabling it to take flight in the darkness of night in search of prey. Manananggals are known to target pregnant women, using their elongated, proboscis-like tongues to extract foetuses or blood from unsuspecting victims while they sleep. They are said to also have a penchant for newlyweds, couples in love and newborns. When the separated lower torso is left vulnerable, it can be destroyed through various means such as applying salt, crushed garlic, fire, or ash. This makes it impossible for the upper torso to reattach itself and, as a result, the Manananggal dies by sunrise.

ORYOL: In Bicolano mythology, the Oryol or Oriol is a renowned figure known as the snake daughter of the lord Asuang, who, among many other characteristics, possess the ability to appear and vanish at will. Her primary objective, however, is to allure men with her irresistible charm and influence them, resulting in countless tales of her enchanting prowess. In her human guise, she assumes the form of a captivating maiden with flowing black hair and flawless, fair skin and a melodious voice that adds to her supernatural magnetism. However, her true form is that of a colossal, multi-coloured serpent, with blindingly shimmering scales.

The Oriol also plays a significant role in the Bicolano epic, *Ibalong*, which consists of sixty stanzas and draws inspiration from the Indian Hindu epics *Ramayana* and *Mahabharata*. Within these narratives, the Oriol is depicted as a pivotal character who aids in bringing peace to the land by vanquishing the menacing beasts of Ibalong alongside the warrior hero, Handiong.

According to the epic, initially, Handiong attempted to ensnare the Oriol, but she cunningly employed her enchanting voice, aided by the *Magindara* (flesh-eating mermaids), to lure him and his companions to their potential demise. Despite surviving the ordeal, Handiong harboured a thirst for vengeance against Oriol and the Magindara, leading to their imprisonment in a vast cave.

Within the confines of the cave, Oriol and Handiong engaged in a fierce battle, showcasing their formidable combat skills. However, their confrontation concluded in a stalemate, ultimately giving rise to an unexpected outcome of mutual respect and admiration blossoming between them. United in love, Oriol and Handiong emerged as the rulers of Ibalon, steering the land towards prosperity.

Bibliography

Alvaro Limos, M. (2020, April 18). *Albularyo: Why 'Magic' healing still prevails in the Philippines.* Esquire PH. https://www.esquiremag.ph/long-reads/features/albularyo-origins-and-practices-philippines-a00293-20200418-lfrm

Clark, J. (2022a, June 2). *Handyong & Oryol: A Bicol folk tale of love and redemption.* The Aswang Project. https://www.aswangproject.com/handyong-oryol/

Clark, J. (2022b, June 2). *The many names of Philippine shamans & healers.* The Aswang Project. https://www.aswangproject.com/philippine-shamans/

Clark, J. (2022c, June 3). *Ghouls in Philippine folklore.* The Aswang Project. https://www.aswangproject.com/philippine-ghouls/

Lynch, F. X. (1949). *Ang mga aswang: A Bicol Belief.*

Ramos, M. D. (1971). *The Aswang complex in Philippine folklore.* https://openlibrary.org/books/OL1691349M/The_Aswang_complex_in_Philippine_folklore

Acknowledgements

The Secret Lives of OFWs would have likely remained a secret if not for the love and support of family and friends who have given me the inspiration to write and keep going. I can't thank you all enough!

To Merle Tagasa and Eugenio Tagasa, my parents, for somehow finding each other to craft the precise genetic blend that has shaped me into the neurotic, macabre loving, Bicolana writer I am today. I hope, I've made you proud, or at least left you both mildly amused with my literary accomplishment.

To Ricky Tagasa, for breathing wonderful life into these characters with your art and talent. You are a Godsend!

To the Mallorca family, my grandparents Miguel and Severina Mallorca. My uncles, Ruben, Ruding, Miguel, and my aunt Genie, for being a source of inspiration and a delightful well of quirky characters.

The Misolas clan for being a valuable source of Bicolano stories and anecdotes. Special mention to Julius and Arnie Misolas for becoming the unexpected bards of the family and to Alden Misolas for always getting the tribe together and providing ample amounts of alcohol during these unintentional research sessions. I look forward to more spontaneous fam jams!

To Jen Tagasa and Norman Wilwayco, for believing in my stories and for always encouraging me to get it out there.

To Kuo-Yu Lian, for generously sharing your valuable guidance, knowledge, and expertise.

To Denis Claves, my boss, for allowing me the time off I needed to complete my stories and make my manuscript deadline. See? I kept my promise about having you in the book. Haha, char.

To the Filipinas Heritage Library at the Ayala Museum, for being a wonderful resource place, and writing space. Thank you to the lovely and gracious librarians for always being helpful.

To the province of Albay, my muse. For constantly igniting my imagination, my constant source of enchantment, pinangat and, of course, for being the mythical home of Mt Mayon.

To my fur babies, Mr Freddiekins Von Disco Jinglefeet aka Mr Fred, Michael Bay aka MB, for constantly reminding me that there's always time for a cuddle break. And, to Scrappulees Mulligan aka Scrappy, for sending me an owl, helping me get over my grief, and letting me know, that everything will be okay.

To this special group of people, thank you for showing up and for giving me the encouragement I needed, especially during the times when I've felt hopeless and close to giving up. Many of you may not have realized it, but your love and support kept me going. One day, we'll all celebrate together and there will be a lot of dancing. I promise. With much love and gratitude to Tina Samuel, Megan Pickett, Janet Blasius, Shauna Teiko Mcdermott, and Graeme Renaud.

Most of all, to Bret Lane Benson, my long-suffering husband, for continuing to love me even at my craziest. Thank you for being so gracious, kind, understanding, and patient throughout the process of completing this book. You are my rock, I love you!

And to you, dear reader, thank you for joining me on this journey. I hope you've enjoyed the places we've visited and the characters you've encountered along the way. I hope to do more of this in the future and would love to hear your thoughts on what stories and which characters you'd like to read more about. You can follow me on Facebook **@IstoryaniJet** and on Instagram **@officiallyjet**. I look forward to connecting with you.